I0653790

The Story of Ab

Also from Westphalia Press
westphaliapress.org

The Story of Ab

A Tale of the Time of the Cave Man

by Stanley Waterloo

WESTPHALIA PRESS
An Imprint of Policy Studies Organization

The Story of Ab: A Tale of the Time of the Cave Man
All Rights Reserved © 2018 by Policy Studies Organization

Westphalia Press
An imprint of Policy Studies Organization
1527 New Hampshire Ave., NW
Washington, D.C. 20036
info@ipsonet.org

ISBN-13: 978-1-63391-647-0
ISBN-10: 1-63391-647-2

Cover design by Jeffrey Barnes:
jbarnesbook.design

Daniel Gutierrez-Sandoval, Executive Director
PSO and Westphalia Press

Updated material and comments on this edition
can be found at the Westphalia Press website:
www.westphaliapress.org

THE STORY OF AB

THE STORY OF AB

A TALE OF THE TIME
OF THE CAVE MAN

BY

STANLEY WATERLOO

**Author of "A Man and a Woman,"
"An Odd Situation," etc.**

GARDEN CITY   NEW YORK
DOUBLEDAY, PAGE & COMPANY
1912

Copyright, 1897, by Way & Williams

INTRODUCTION.

THIS is the story of Ab, a man of the Age of Stone, who lived so long ago that we cannot closely fix the date, and who loved and fought well.

In his work the author has been cordially assisted by some of the ablest searchers of two continents into the life history of prehistoric times. With characteristic helpfulness and interest, these already burdened students have aided and encouraged him, and to them he desires to express his sense of profound obligation and his earnest thanks.

Once only does the writer depart from accepted theories of scientific research. After an at least long-continued study of existing evidence and information relating to the Stone Ages, the conviction grew upon him that the mysterious gap supposed by scientific teachers to divide Paleolithic from Neolithic man never really existed. No convulsion of nature, no new race of human beings is needed to explain the difference between the relics of Paleolithic and Neolithic strugglers. Growth, experiment, adaptation, discovery, inevitable in man, sufficiently account for all the relatively swift changes from one form of primitive life to another more advanced, from the time of chipped to that of polished implements. Man has been, from the beginning, under the never resting, never hastening, forces of evolution. The earth from which he sprang holds the record of his transformations in her peat-beds, her buried caverns and her rocky fastnesses. The eternal laws change man, but they themselves do not change.

Ab and Lightfoot and others of the cave people whose story is told in the tale which follows the author cannot disown. He has shown them as they were. Hungry and cold, they slew the fierce beasts which were scarcely more savage than they, and were fed and clothed by their flesh and fur. In the caves of the earth the cave men and their families were safely sheltered. Theirs were the elemental wants and passions. They were swayed by love, in some form at least, by jealousy, fear, revenge, and by the memory of benefits and wrongs. They cherished their young; they fought desperately with the beasts of their time, and with each other, and, when their brief, turbulent lives were ended, they passed into silence, but not into oblivion. The old Earth carefully preserved their story, so that we, their children, may read it now.

S. W.

CONTENTS.

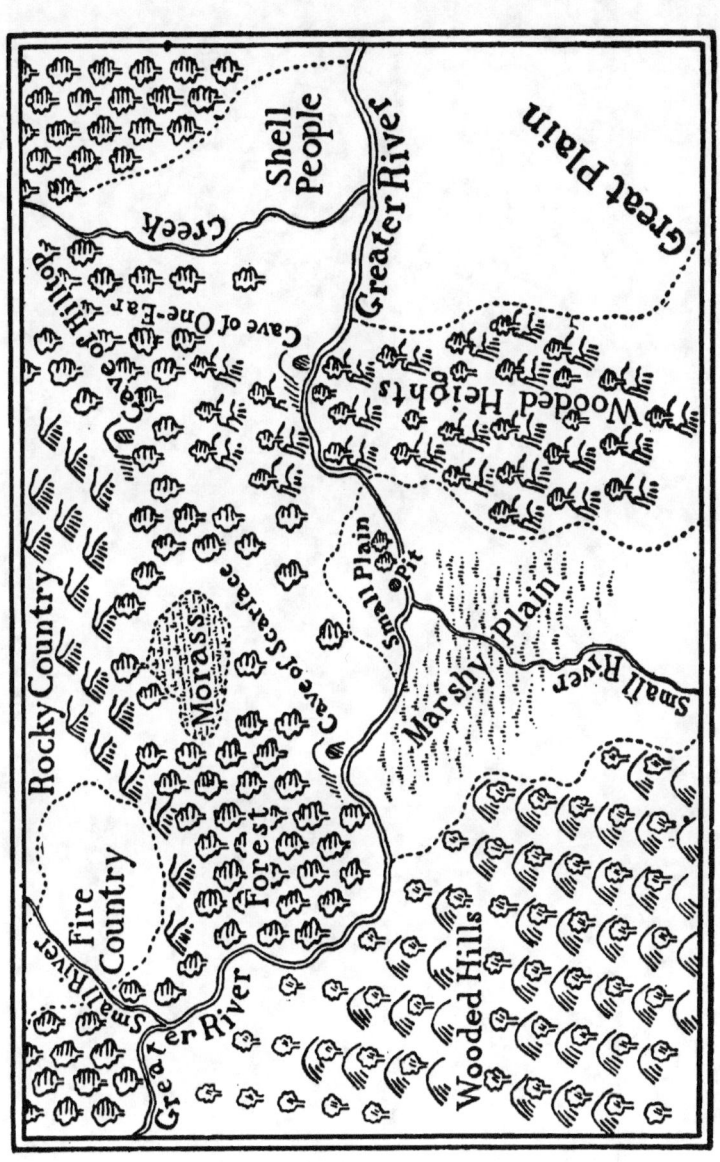

THE STORY OF AB.

CHAPTER I.

THE BABE IN THE WOODS.

DRIFTED beech leaves had made a soft, clean bed in a little hollow in a wood. The wood was beside a river, the trend of which was toward the east. There was an almost precipitous slope, perhaps a hundred and fifty feet from the wood, downward to the river. The wood itself, a sort of peninsula, was small in extent and partly isolated from the greater forest back of it by a slight clearing. Just below the wood, or, in fact, almost in it and near the crest of the rugged bank, the mouth of a small cave was visible. It was so blocked with stones as to leave barely room for the entrance of a human being. The little couch of beech leaves already referred to was not many yards from the cave.

On the leafy bed rolled about and kicked up his short legs in glee a little brown babe. It was evident that he could not walk yet and his lack of length and width and thickness indicated what might be a babe not more than a year of age, but, despite his apparent youth, this man-child seemed content thus left alone, while his grip on the twigs which had fallen into his bed was strong, as he was strong, and he was breaking them delightedly. Not only was the hair upon his head at least twice as long as that of the average year-old child of to-day, but there were downy indications upon his arms and legs, and his general aspect was a swart and rugged one. He was about as far from a weakly child in appearance as could be well imagined and he was about as jolly a looking baby, too, as one could wish to see. He was laughing and cooing as he kicked about among the beech leaves and looked upward at the blue sky. His dress has not yet been alluded to and an apology for the negligence may be found in the fact that he had no dress. He wore nothing. He was a baby of the time of the cave men; of the closing period of the age of chipped stone instruments; the epoch of mild climate; the ending of one great animal group and the beginning of another; the time when the mammoth, the rhinoceros, the great cave tiger and cave bear, the huge elk, reindeer and aurochs and urus and hosts of little horses, fed or gamboled in the same forests and plains, with much discretion as to relative distances from each other.

It was some time ago, no matter how many thousands of years, when the child—they called him Ab—lay there, naked, upon his bed of beech leaves. It may be said, too, that there existed for him every chance for a lively and interesting existence. There was prospect that he would be engaged in running away from something or running after something during most of his life. Times were not dull for humanity in the age of stone. The children had no lack of things to interest, if not always to amuse, them, and neither had the men and women. And this is the truthful story of the boy Ab and his playmates and of what happened when he grew to be a man.

It is well to speak here of the river. The stream has been already mentioned as flowing to the eastward. It did not flow in that direction regularly; its course was twisted and diverted, and there were bays and inlets and rapids between precipices, and islands and wooded peninsulas, and then the river merged

into a lake of miles in extent, the waters con-
verging into the river again.   So it was that
the banks in one place might form a height
and in another merge evenly into a densely
wooded forest or a wide plain.   It was so, too,
that these conditions might exist opposite each
other.   Thus the woodland might face the
plain, or the precipice some vast extending
marsh.

To speak further of this river it may be mentioned, incidentally, that to-day its upper
reaches still exist and that the relatively small
stream remaining is called the Thames.   Beside and across it lies the greatest city in the
world and its mouth is upon what is called the
English Channel.   At the time when the baby,
Ab, slept that afternoon in his nest in the
beech leaves this river was not called the
Thames, it was only called the Running Water,
to distinguish it from the waters of the coast.
It did not empty into the British Channel, for
the simple and sufficient reason that there was
no such channel at the time.   Where now
exists that famous passage which makes islands
of Great Britain, where, tossed upon the
choppy waves, the travelers of the world are
seasick, where Drake and Howard chased the

Great Armada to the Northern seas and where, to-day, the ships of the nations are steered toward a social and commercial center, was then good, solid earth crowned with great forests, and the present little tail end of a river was part of a great affluent of the Rhine, the German river famous still, but then with a a size and sweep worth talking of.   Then the Thames and the Elbe and Weser, into which tumbled a thousand smaller streams, all went to feed what is now the Rhine, and that then tremendous river held its course through dense forests and deep gorges until it reached broad plains, where the North Sea is to-day, and blended finally with the Northern Ocean.

The trees which stood upon the bank of the great river, or which could be seen in the far distance beyond the marsh or plain, were not all the same as now exist.   There was still a distinctive presence of the towering conifers, something such as are represented in the redwood forests of California to-day, or, in other forms, in some Australian woods. There was a suggestion of the fernlike but gigantic age of growth of the distant past, the past when the earth's surface was yet warm and its air misty, and there was an exuberance of all plant and forest growth, something compared with which the growth in the same latitude, just now, would make, it may be, but a stunted showing. It is wonderful, though, the close resemblance between most of the trees of the cave man's age, so many tens of thousands of years ago, and the trees most common to the temperate zone to-day. The peat bogs and the caverns and the strata of deposits in a host of places tell truthfully what trees grew in this distant time. Already the oak and beech and walnut and butternut and hazel reared their graceful forms aloft, and the ground beneath their spreading branches was strewn with the store of nuts which gave a portion of food for many of the beasts and for man as well. The ash and the yew were there, tough and springy of fiber and destined in the far future to become famous in song and story, because they would furnish the wood from which was made the weapon of the bowman. The maple was there with all its symmetry. There was the elm, the dogged and beautiful tree-thing of to-day, which so clings to life and flourishes in the midst of unwholesome city surroundings and makes the human hive so much the better. There were the pines, the sycamore, the foxwood and dogwood, and lime and laurel and poplar and elder and willow, and the cherry and crab apple and others of the fruit-bearing kind, since so developed that they are great factors in man's subsistence now. It was a time of plenty which was riotous. There remained, too, a vestige of the animal as well as of the vegetable life of the remoter ages. There were strange and dangerous creatures which came sometimes up the river from its inlet into the ocean. Such events had been matters of interest, not to say of anxiety, to Ab's ancestors.

The baby lying there among the beech leaves tired, finally, of its cooing and twig-snapping and slept the sleep of dreamless early childhood. He slept happily and noiselessly, but when he at last awoke his demeanor showed a change. He had nothing to distract him, unless it might be the breaking of twigs again. He had no toys, and, being hungry, he began to yell. So far as can be learned from early data, babies, when hungry, have always yelled. And, of old, as to-day, when a baby yelled, the woman who had borne it was likely to appear at once upon the scene. Ab's mother came running lightly from the river bank toward where the youngster lay. She was worthy of at†ention as she ran, and this is but a bungling attempt at a description of her and of her dress.

It should be explained here, with much care and caution, that the mother of Ab moved in the best and most exclusive circles of the time. She belonged to the aristocracy and, it may be added, regarding this fine lady personally, that she had the weakness of paying much attention to her dress. She was what might properly be called a leader of society, though society was at the time somewhat attenuated, families living, generally, some miles apart, and various obstacles, chiefly in the form of large, man-eating animals, complicating the matter of paying calls. As for the calls themselves, they were nearly as often aggressive as social, and there is a certain degree of difference between the vicious use of a flint ax and the leaving of a card with a bending lackey. But all this doesn't matter. The mother of Ab belonged to the very cream of the cream, and was dressed accordingly. Her garb was elegant but simple; it had, first, the one great merit, that it could easily be put on or taken off. It was sustained with but a single knot, a bow-knot—they had learned to make a bow-knot and other knots in the stone age, for, because of the manual requirements for living, they were cleverer fumblers with their fingers than we are now— and the lady here described had tied her knot in a manner not to be excelled by any other woman in all the fiercely beast-ranged coun-tryside.

The gown itself was of a quality to please the eye of the most carping. It was made from the skins of wolverines, and was drawn in loosely about the waist by a tied band, but was really sustained by a strip of the skin which encircled the left shoulder and back and breast. This left the right arm free from all encumbrance, a matter of some impor-tance, for to be right-handed was a quality of the cave man as of the man to-day. We should have a grudge against them for this carelessness, and should, may be, form an ambidextrous league, improving upon the past and teaching and forcing young children to use each hand alike.

The garment of wolverine skins, sewed neatly together with thread of sinews, was all the young mother wore. Thus hanging from the shoulder and fully encircling her, it reached from the waist to about half way down between the hips and the knees. It was as delightful a gown as ever was contrived by ambitious modiste or mincing male designer in these modern times. It fitted with a free and easy looseness and its colors were such as blended smoothly and kindly with the complexion of its wearer. The fur of the wolverine was a mixed black and white, but neither black nor white is the word to use. The black was not black; it was only a swart sort of color, and the white was not white; it was but a dingy, lighter contrast to the darker surface beside it. Yet the combination was rather good. There was enough of difference to catch the eye and not enough of glaringness to offend it. The mother of Ab would be counted by a wise observer as the possessor of good taste. Still, dress is a small matter. There is something to say about the cave mother aside from the mere description of her gown.

CHAPTER II.

MAN AND HYENA.

IT is but an act of simple gallantry and justice to assert that the cave woman had a certain unhampered swing of movement which the modern woman often lacks. Without any reflection upon the blessed woman of to-day, it must be said truthfully that she can neither leap a creek nor surmount some such obstacle as a monster tree trunk with a close approach to the ease and grace of this mother who came bounding through the forest. There was nothing unknowing or hesitant about her movements. She ran swiftly and leaped lightly when occasion came. She was lithe as the panther and as careless of where her brown feet touched the ground.

The woman had physical charms. She was of about the average size of womanhood as we see it embodied now, but her waist was not compressed at an unseemly angle, and much resembled in its contour that of the Venus of Milo which has become such a stock ex-

ample of the healthfully symmetrical. Her
hair was brown and long. It was innocent of
knot or coil or braid, and was transfixed by
no abatis of dangerous pins. It was not
parted but was thrown straight backward over
the head and hung down fairly and far between
brown shoulders. It was a fine head of hair;
there could be no question about that. It had
gloss and color. Captious critics, reasoning
from the standpoint of another age, might
think it needed combing, but that is only a
matter of opinion. It was tangled together
in a compact and fluffy mass, and so did not
wander into the woman's eyes, which was a
good thing and a great convenience, for bright
eyes and unobstructed vision were required in
those lively days.

The face of this lady showed, at a glance,
that no cosmetic had ever been relied upon to
give it an artificial charm. As a matter of fact
it would have been difficult to use cosmetics
upon that face in the modern way, for there
was a suggestion of something more than down
upon the countenance, and there were certain
irregularities of facial outline so prominent that
such details as the little matter of complexion
must be trifling. The eyes were deep set and

small, the nose was short and thick and possessed a certain vagueness of outline not easy of description. The upper lip was excessively long and the under lip protruding. The chin was well defined and firm. The mouth was rather wide, and the teeth were strong and even, and as white as any ivory ever seen. Such was the face, and there may be added some details of interest about the figure. The arms of this fascinating woman were perfectly proportioned. They were adapted to the times and were very beautiful. Down each of them from shoulder to elbow ran a strip of short dark hair. From either hand ran upward to the elbow another strip of hair, and the two, meeting at the elbow, formed a delightful little tuft reminding one of what is known as a "widow's peak," or that little point which grows down so charmingly on an occasional woman's forehead. Her biceps were tremendous, as must necessarily be the case with a lady accustomed to swing from limb to limb along the treetops. Her thumb was nearly as long as her fingers, and the palms of her hands were hard. Her legs were like her arms in their degree of muscular development and hairy adornment. She had beautiful feet.

It is to be admitted that her heels projected a trifle more than is counted the ideal thing at the present day, and that her big toe and all the other toes were very much in evidence, but there is not one woman in ten thousand now who could as handily pick up objects with her toes as could the mother of the baby Ab. She was as brown as a nut, with the tan of a half tropical summer, and as healthy a creature, from tawny head to backward sloping heel, as ever trod a path in the world's history. This was the quality of the lady who came so swiftly to learn the nature of her offspring's trouble. Ladies of that day attended, as a rule, to the wants of their own children. A wet nurse was a thing unknown and a dry one as unthought of. This was good for the children.

The woman made a dive into the little hollow and picked the babe from its nest of leaves and tossed him up lightly, and at once his crying ceased, and his little brown arms went around her neck, and he cooed and prattled in very much the same fashion as does a babe of the present time. He was content, all in a moment, yet some noise must have aroused him, for, as it chanced, there was great need

that this particular babe at this particular
moment should have awakened and cried aloud
for his mother. This was made evident immediately. As the woman tossed him aloft in
her arms and cuddled him again there came a
sound to her ears which made her leap like
some wilder creature of the forest up to a little
vantage ground. She turned her head, and
then—you should have seen the woman!

Very nearly above them swung down one of
the branches of a great beech tree. The
mother threw the child into the hollow of her
left arm, and leaped upward a yard to catch
the branch with her right hand. So she hung
dangling. Then, instantly, holding him firmly
by one arm in her left hand, she lowered the
child between her legs and clasped them about
him closely. And then, had it been your fortune to be born in those times, you might have
seen good climbing. With both her strong
arms free, this vigorous matron ran up the
stout beech limb which depended downward
from the great bole of the tree until she was
twenty feet above the ground, and then, lifting
herself into a comfortable place, in a moment
was sitting there at ease, her legs and one arm
coiled about the big branch and a smaller up-

standing one, while the other arm held the brown babe close to her bosom.

This charming lady of the period had reached her perch in the beech tree top none too soon. Even as she swung herself into place upon the huge bough, there came rushing across the space beneath, snarling, smelling and seeking, a brute as foul and dangerous as could be imagined for mother and son upon the ground. It was of a dirty dun color, mottled and striped with a lighter but still dingy hue. It had a black, hoggish nose, but there were fangs in its great jaws. It resembled a huge wolf, save as to its massiveness and club countenance. It was one of the monster hyenas of the time, a beast which must have been as dangerous to the men then living as any animal except the cave tiger and the cave bear. Its degenerate posterity, as they shuffle uneasily back and forth when caged to-day, are perhaps not less foul of aspect, but are relatively pygmies. Doubtless the brute had scented the sleeping babe, and, snarling aloud in its search, had waked it, inducing the cry which proved the child's salvation.

The beast scented immediately the prey above him and leaped upward ferociously and vainly. Was the woman thus beset thus holding herself aloft and with her child upon one arm in a state of sickening anxiety? Hardly! She but encircled the supporting branch the closer, and laughed aloud. She even poked one bare foot down at the leaping beast, and waved her leg in provocation. At the same time there was no doubt that she was beset. Furthermore she was hungry, and so she raised her voice, and sent out through the forest a strange call, a quavering minor wail, but something to be heard at a great distance. There was no delay in the response, for delays were dangerous when cave men lived. The call was answered instantly and the answering cry was repeated as she called again, the sound of the reply approaching near and nearer all the time. All at once the manner of her calling changed; it was an appeal no longer; it was a conversation, an odd, clucking, penetrating speech in the shortest of sentences. She was telling of the situation. There was prompt reply; the voice seemed suddenly higher in the air and then came, swinging easily from branch to branch along the treetops, the father of Ab, a person who felt a natural and agressive interest in what was going on.

To describe the cave man it is, it may be, best of all to say that he was the woman over again, only stronger, longer limbed and deeper chested, firmer of jaw and more grim of countenance. He was dressed almost as she was. From his broad shoulder hung a cloak of the skin of some wild beast but the cord which tied it was a stout one, and in the belt thus formed was stuck a weapon of such quality as men have rarely carried since. It was a stone ax; an ax heavier than any battle-ax of mediæval times, its haft a scant three feet in length, inclosing the ax through a split in the tough wood, all being held in place by a taut and hardened mass of knotted sinews. It was a fearful weapon, but one only to be wielded by such a man as this, one with arms almost as mighty as those of the gorilla.

The man sat himself upon the limb beside his wife and child. The two talked together in their clucking language for a moment or two, but few words were wasted. Words had not their present abundance in those days; action was everything. The man was hungry, too, and wanted to get home as soon as possible. He had secured food, which was awaiting them, and this slight, annoying episode of the day must be ended promptly. He clambered easily up the tree and wrenched off a deadened limb at least two yards in length, then tumbling back again and passing his wife and child along the main branch, he swung down to where the leaping beast could almost reach him. The heavy club he carried gave him an advantage. With a whistling sweep, as the hyena leaped upward in its ravenous folly, came this huge club crashing against the thick skull, a blow so fair and stark and strong that the stunned beast fell backward upon the ground, and then, down, lightly as any monkey, dropped the cave man. The huge stone ax went crashing into the brain of the quivering brute, and that was the end of the incident. Mother and child leaped down together, and the man and woman went chattering toward their cave. This was not a particularly eventful day with them; they were accustomed to such things.

They went strolling off through the beech glades, the strong, hairy, heavy-jawed man, the muscular but more lightly built woman and the child, perched firmly and chattering blithely upon her shoulder as they walked, or, rather, half trotted along the river side and toward the cave. They were light of foot and light of thought, but there was ever that almost unconscious alertness appertaining to their time. Their flexible ears twitched, and turned, now forward now backward, to catch the slightest sound. Their nostrils were open for dangerous scents, or for the scent of that which might give them food, either animal or vegetable, and as for the eyes, well, they were the sharpest existent within the history of the human race. They were keen of vision at long distance and close at hand, and ever were they in motion, swiftly turned sidewise this way and that, peering far ahead or looking backward to note what enemies of the wood might be upon the trail. So, swiftly along the glade and ever alert, went the father and mother of Ab, carrying the strong child with them.

There came no new alarm, and soon the cave was reached, though on the way there was a momentary deviation from the path, to gather up the nuts and berries the woman had found in the afternoon while the babe was lying sleeping. The fruitage was held in a great leaf, a pliant thing pulled together at the edges, tied stoutly with a strand of tough grass, and mak-

ing a handy pouch containing a quart or two
of the food, which was the woman's contribu-
tion to the evening meal. As for the father,
he had more to offer, as was evident when the
cave was reached.

The man and woman crept through the
narrow entrance and stood erect in a recess
in the rocks twenty feet square, at least, and
perhaps fifteen feet in height. Looking upward one could see a gleam of light from the
outer world. The orifice through which the
light came was the chimney, dug downward
with much travail from the level of the land
above. Directly underneath the opening was
the fireplace, for men had learned thoroughly
the use of fire, and had even some fancies as
to getting rid of smoke. There were smoldering embers upon the hearth, embers of the
hardest of wood, the wood which would pre-
serve a fire for the greatest length of time, for
the cave man had neither flint and steel nor
matches, and when a fire expired it was a matter of some difficulty to secure a flame again.
On this occasion there was no trouble. The
embers were beaten up easily into glowing
coals and twigs and dry dead limbs cast upon
them made soon a roaring flame. As the

cave was lighted the proprietor pointed laughingly to the abundance of meat he had secured.
It was food of the finest sort and in such
quantity that even this stalwart being's strength
must have been exceptionally tested in bringing the burden to the cave. It was something
in quality for an epicure of the day and there
was enough of it to make the cave man's
family easy for a week, at least. It was a
hind quarter of a wild horse.

CHAPTER III.

A FAMILY DINNER.

DESPITE the hyena and baby incident, the day had been a satisfactory one for this cave family. Of course, had the woman failed to reach just when she did the hollow in which her babe was left there would have come a tragedy in the extinction of a young and promising cave child, and the two would have been mourning, as even wild beasts mourn for their lost young. But there was little reversion to past possibilities in the minds of the cave people. The couple were not worrying over what might have been. The mother had found food of one sort in abundance, and the father's fortune had been royal. He had tossed a rock from a precipice a hundred feet in height down into a passing herd of the little wild horses, and great luck had followed, for one of them had been killed, and so this was a holiday in the cave. The man and wife were at ease and had each an appetite.

The nuts gathered by the woman were

tossed in a heap among the ashes and live coals were raked upon them, and the popping which followed showed how well they were being roasted. A sturdy twig, two yards in length and sharpened at the end, was utilized by the man in cooking the strips of meat cut from the haunch of the wild horse and very savory were the odors that filled the cave. There was the faint perfume of the crackling nuts and there was the fragrant beneficence of the broiling meat. There are no definite records upon the subject; the chef of to-day can give you no information on the point, but there is reason to believe that a steak from the wild horse of the time was something admirable. There is a sort of maxim current in this age, in civilized rural communities, to the effect that those quadrupeds are good to eat which ''chew the cud or part the hoof.'' The horse of to-day is a creature with but one toe to each leg—we all know that—but the horse of the cave man's time had only lately parted with the split hoof, and so was fairly edible, even according to the modern standard.

The father and mother of Ab were not more than two years past their honeymoon. They, in their way, were glad that their union had been so blest and that a lusty man-child was rolling about and crowing and cooing upon the earthen floor of the cave. They lived from hand to mouth, and from day to day, and this day had been a good one. They were there together, man, woman and child. They had warmth and food. The entrance to the cave was barred so that no monster of the period might enter. They could eat and sleep with a certainty of the perfect digestion which followed such a life as theirs and with a certainty of all peace for the moment. Even the child mumbled heartily, though not yet very strongly, at the delicious meat of the little horse, and, the meal ended, the two lay down upon a mass of leaves which made their bed, and the child lay snuggled and warm within reach of them. The aristocracy of the time had gone to sleep.

There was silence in the cave, but, outside, the world was not so still. The night was not always one of silence in the cave man's time. The hours of darkness were those when the creature which walked upon two legs was no longer gliding through the forest with ready club or spear, and when those creatures which used four legs instead of two, especially the defense-less, felt more at ease than in the daytime. The grass-eating animals emerged from the forest into the plateaus and upon the low plains along the river side and the flesh-eaters began again their hunting. It was a time of wild life, and of wild death, for out of the abundance much was taken; there were nightly tragedies, and the beasts of prey were as glutted as the urus or the elk which fed on the sweet grasses. It was but a matter of difference in diet and in the manner of doing away with one life which must be sacrificed to support another. There was liveliness at night with the queer thing, man, out of the way, and brutes and beasts of many sorts, taking their chances together, were happier with him absent. They could not understand him, and liked him not, though the great-clawed and sharp-toothed ones had a vast desire to eat him. He was a disturbing element in the community of the plain and forest.

And, while all this play of life and death went on outside, the three people, the man, woman and child, in the cave slept as soundly as sleep the drunken or the just. They were full-fed and warm and safe. No beast of a size greater than that of a lank wolf or sinewy wildcat could enter the cave through the narrow entrance between the heaped-up rocks, and of these, as of any other dangerous beast, there was none which would face what barred even the narrow passage, for it was fire. Just at the entrance the all-night fire of knots and hardest wood smoked, flamed and smoldered and flickered, and then flamed again, and held the passageway securely. No animal that ever lived, save man, has ever dared the touch of fire. It was the cave man's guardian.

CHAPTER IV.

AB AND OAK.

Such were the father and mother of Ab, and such was the boy himself. His surroundings have not been indicated with all the definiteness desirable, because of the lack of certain data, but, in a general way, the degree of his birth, the manner of his rearing and the natural aspects of his estate have been described. That the young man had a promising future could not admit of doubt. He was the first-born of an important family of a great race and his inheritance had no boundaries. Just where the possessions of the Ab family began or where they terminated no bird nor beast nor human being could tell. The estates of the family extended from the Mediterranean to the Arctic Ocean and there were no dividing lines. Of course, something depended upon the existence or non-existence of a stronger cave family somewhere else, but that mattered not. And the babe grew into a sturdy youth, just as grow the boys of to-day, and had his friendships and adventures. He did not attend the public schools—the school system was what might reasonably be termed inefficient in his time—nor did he attend a private school, for the private schools were weak, as well, but he did attend the great school of Nature from the moment he opened his eyes in the morning until he closed them at night. Of his schoolboy days and his friendships and his various affairs, this is the immediate story.

The father and mother of Ab as has, it is hoped, been made apparent, were strong people, intelligent up to the grade of the time and worthy of regard in many ways. The two could fairly hold their own, not only against the wild beasts, but against any other cave pair, should the emergency arise. They had names, of course. The name of Ab's father was One-Ear, the sequence of an incident occurring when he was very young, an accidental and too intimate acquaintance with a species of wildcat which infested the region and from which the babe had been rescued none too soon. The name of Ab's mother was Red-Spot, and she had been so called because of a not unsightly but conspicuous birthmark appearing on her left shoulder. As to ancestry, Ab's father could distinctly remember his own grandfather as the old gentleman had appeared just previous to his consumption by a monstrous bear, and Red-Spot had some vague remembrance of her own grandmother.

As for Ab's own name, it came from no personal mark or peculiarity or as the result of any particular incident of his babyhood. It was merely a convenient adaptation by his parents of a childish expression of his own, a labial attempt to say something. His mother had mimicked his babyish prattlings, the father had laughed over the mimicry, and, almost unconsciously, they referred to their baby afterward as "Ab," until it grew into a name which should be his for life. There was no formal early naming of a child in those days; the name eventually made itself, and that was all there was to it. There was, for instance, a child living not many miles away, destined to be a future playmate and ally of Ab, who, though of nearly the same age, had not yet been named at all. His title, when he finally attained it, was merely Oak. This was not because he was straight as an oak, or because he had an acorn birthmark, but because adjoining the cave where he was born stood a great oak with spreading limbs, from one of which was dangled a rude cradle, into which the babe was tied, and where he would be safe from all attacks during the absence of his parents on such occasions as they did not wish the burden of carrying him about. "Rock-a-by-baby upon the tree-top" was often a reality in the time of the cave men.

Ab was fortunate in being born at a reasonably comfortable stage of the world's history. He had a decent prospect as to clothing and shelter, and there was abundance of food for those brave enough or ingenious enough to win it. The climate was not enervating. There were cold times for the people of the epoch and, in their seasons, harsh and chilling winds swept over bare and chilling glaciers, though a semi-tropical landscape was all about. So suddenly had come the change from frigid cold to moderate warmth, that the vast fields of ice once moving southward were not thawed to their utmost depths even when rank vegetation and a teeming life had sprung up in the now European area, and so it came that, in some places, cold, white monuments and glittering plateaus still showed

themselves amid the forest and fed the tumbling streams which made the rivers rushing to
the ocean.   There were days of bitter cold in
winter and sultry heat in summer.

It may fairly be borne in mind of this child
Ab that he was somewhat different from the
child of to-day, and nearer the quadruped in
his manner of swift development.   The puppy
though delinquent in the matter of opening it's
eyes, waddles clumsily upon its legs very early
in its career.   Ab, of course, had his eyes
open from the beginning, and if the babe of
to-day were to stand upright as soon as Ab
did, his mother would be the proudest creature
going and his father, at the club, would be a
thing intolerable. It must be admitted, though,
that neither One-Ear nor Red-Spot manifested
an extraordinary degree of enthusiasm over
the precociousness of their first-born.   He was
not, for the time, remarkable, and parents of
the day were less prone than now to spoiling
children.   Ab's layette had been of beech
leaves, his bed had been of beech leaves,
and a beech twig, supple and stinging, had
already been applied to him when he mis-
behaved himself.   As he grew older his acquaintance with it would be more familiar.

Strict disciplinarians in their way, though
affectionate enough after their own fashion,
were the parents of the time.

The existence of this good family of the day
continued without dire misadventure. Ab at
nine years of age was a fine boy. There
could be no question about that. He was as
strong as a young gibbon, and, it must be admitted, in certain characteristics would have
conveyed to the learned observer of to-day a
suggestion of that same animal. His eyes
were bright and keen and his mouth and nose
were worth looking at. His nose was broad,
with nostrils aggressively prominent, and as
for his mouth, it was what would be called
to-day excessively generous in its proportions
for a boy of his size. But it did not lack expression. His lips could quiver at times, or
become firmly set, and there was very much
of what might, even then, be called ''manli-
ness'' in the general bearing of the sturdy little
cave child. He had never cried much when
a babe—cave children were not much addicted
to crying, save when very hungry—and he
had grown to his present stature, which was
not very great, with a healthfulness and general manner of buoyancy all the time. He

was as rugged a child of his age as could be found between the shore that lay long leagues westward of what is now the western point of Ireland and anywhere into middle Europe. He had begun to have feelings and hopes and ambitions, too. He had found what his surroundings meant. He had at least done one thing well. He had made well-received advances toward a friend; and a friend is a great thing for a boy, when he is another boy of about the same age. This friendship was not quite commonplace.

Ab, who could climb like a young monkey, laid most casually the foundation for this companionship which was to affect his future life. He had scrambled, one day, up a tree standing near the cave, and, climbing out along a limb near its top, had found a comfortable resting-place, and there upon the swaying bough was "teetering" comfortably, when something in another tree, further up the river, caught his sharp eye. It was a dark mass,—it might have been anything caught in a treetop,—but the odd part of it was that it was "teetering" just as he was. Ab watched the object for a long time curiously, and finally decided that it must be another boy, or perhaps a girl, who was swaying in the distant tree.   There came to him a vigorous thought.   He resolved to become better acquainted; he resolved dimly, for this was the first time that any idea of further affiliation with anyone had come into his youthful mind.   Of course, it must not be understood that he had been in absolute retirement throughout his young but not uneventful life. Other cave men and women, sometimes accompanied by their children, had visited the cave of One-Ear and Red-Spot and Ab had become somewhat acquainted with other human beings and with what were then the usages of the best hungry society.   He had never, though, become really familiar with anyone save his father and mother and the children which his mother had borne after him, a boy and a girl.   This particular afternoon a sudden boyish yearning came upon him.   He wanted to know who the youth might be who was swinging in the distant tree. He was a resolute young cub, and to determine was to act.

It was rare, particularly in the wooded districts of the country of the cave men, for a boy of nine to go a mile from home alone.

There was danger lurking in every rod and rood, and, naturally, such a boy would not be versed in all woodcraft, nor have the necessary strength of arm for a long arboreal journey, swinging himself along beneath the intermingling branches of close-standing trees. So this departure was, for Ab, a venture something out of the common. But he was strong for his age, and traversed rapidly a considerable distance through the treetops in the direction of what he saw. Once or twice, though, there came exigencies of leaping and grasping aloft to which he felt himself unequal, and then, plucky boy as he was, he slid down the bole of the tree and, looking about cautiously, made a dash across some little glade and climbed again. He had traversed little more than half the distance toward the object he sought when his sharp ears caught the sound of rustling leaves ahead of him. He slipped behind the trunk of the tree into whose top he was clambering and then, reaching out his head, peered forward warily. As he thus ensconced himself, the sound he had heard ceased suddenly. It was odd. The boy was perplexed and somewhat anxious. He could but peer and peer and remain absolutely quiet.

At last his searching watchfulness was re-
warded. He saw a brown protuberance on
the side of a great tree, above where the
branches began, not twoscore yards distant
from him, and that brown protuberance moved
slightly. It was evident that the protuberance was watching him as he was watching it.
He realized what it meant.   There was another boy there! He was not particularly
afraid of another boy and at once came out of
hiding.   The other boy came calmly into view
as well.   They sat there, looking at each
other, each at ease upon a great branch, each
with an arm sustaining himself, each with his
little brown legs dangling carelessly, and each
gazing upon the other with bright eyes evinc-
ing alike watchfulness and curiosity and some
suspicion.   So they sat, perched easily, these
excellent young, monkeyish boys of the time,
each waiting for the other to begin the conversation, just as two boys wait when they
thus meet to-day.   Their talk would not perhaps be intelligible to any professor of lan-
guages in all the present world, but it was a
language, however limited its vocabulary,
which sufficed for the needs of the men and

women and children of the cave time.   It was
Ab who first broke the silence:

"Who are you?" he said.

"I am Oak," responded the other boy.
"Who are you?"

"Me?   Oh, I am Ab."

"Where do you come from?"

"From the cave by the beeches; and where
do you come from?"

"I come from the cave where the river
turns, and I am not afraid of you."

'I am not afraid of you, either," said Ab.

"Let us climb down and get upon that big
rock and throw stones at things in the water,"
said Oak.

"All right," said Ab.

And the two slid, one after the other, down
the great tree trunks and ran rapidly to the
base of a huge rock overtopping the river, and
with sides almost perpendicular, but with crevices and projections which enabled the expert
youngsters to ascend it with ease.   There was
a little plateau upon its top a few yards in area
and, once established there, the boys were
safe from prowling beasts.   And this was the
manner of the first meeting of two who were
destined to grow to manhood together, to be

good companions and have full young lives, howbeit somewhat exciting at times, and to affect each other for joy and sorrow, and good and bad, and all that makes the quality of being.

CHAPTER V.

A GREAT ENTERPRISE.

WHAT always happens when two boys not yet fairly in their 'teens meet, at first aggressively, and then, each gradually overcoming this apprehension of the other, decide upon a close acquaintance and long comradeship? Their talk is firmly optimistic and they constitute much of the world. As for Ab and Oak, when there had come to them an ease in conversation, there dawned gradually upon each the idea that, next to himself, the other was probably the most important personage in the world, fitting companion and confederate of a boy who in an incredibly short space of time was going to become a man and do things on a tremendous scale. Seated upon the rock, a point of ease and vantage, they talked long of what two boys might do, and so earnest did they become in considering their possible great exploits that Ab demanded of Oak that he go with him to his home. This was a serious matter. It was a no slight thing for a boy of that day, allowed a playground within certain limits adjacent to his cave home, to venture far away; but this in Oak's life was a great occasion. It was the first time he had ever met and talked with a boy of his age, and he became suddenly reckless, assenting promptly to Ab's proposal. They ran along the forest paths together toward Ab's cave, clucking in their queer language and utilizing in that short journey most of the brief vocabulary of the day in anticipatory account of what they were going to do.

Ab's father and mother rather approved of Oak. They even went so far as to consent that Ab might pay a return visit upon the succeeding day, though it was stipulated that the father—and this was a demand the mother made—should accompany the boy upon most of the journey. One-Ear knew Oak's father very well. Oak's father, Stripe-Face, was a man of standing in the widely-scattered community. Stripe-Face was so called because in a casual, and, on his part, altogether uninvited encounter with a cave bear when he was a young man, a sweep of the claws of his adversary had plowed furrows down one cheek, leaving scars thereafter which were livid streaks. One-Ear and Stripe-Face were good friends. Sometimes they hunted together; they had fought together, and it was nothing out of the way, and but natural, that Ab and Oak should become companions. So it came that One-Ear went across the forest with his boy the next day and visited the cave of Stripe-Face, and that the two young cubs went out together buoyant and in conquering mood, while the grown men planned something for their own advantage. Certainly the boys matched well. A finer pair of youngsters of eight or nine years of age could hardly be imagined than these two who sallied forth that afternoon. They send very fine boys nowadays to our great high schools in the United States, and to Rugby and Eaton and Harrow in England, but never went forth a finer pair to learn things. No smattering of letters or lore of any printed sort had these rugged youths, but their eyes were piercing as those of the eagle, the grip of their hands was strong, their pace was swift when they ran upon the ground and their course almost as rapid when they swung along the treetops. They were self-possessed and ready and alert and prepared to pass an examination for admission to any university of the time; that is, to any of Nature's universities, where matriculation depended upon prompt conception of existing dangers and the ways of avoiding them, and of all adroitness in attainments which gave food and shelter and safety. Eh! but they were a gallant pair, these two young gentlemen who burst forth, owning the world entirely and feeling a serene confidence in their ability, united, to maintain their rights. And their ambitions soon took a definite turn. They decided that they must kill a horse!

The wild horse of the time, already referred to as esteemed for his edible qualities, was, in the opinion of the cave people, but of moderate value otherwise. He was abundant, ranging in herds of hundreds along the pampas of the great Thames valley, and furnished forth abundant food for man as well as the wild beasts, when they could capture him. His skin, though, was not counted of much worth. Its short hair afforded little warmth in cloak or breech-clout, and the tanned pelt became hard and uncomfortable when it dried after a wetting. Still, there were various uses for this horse's hide. It made fine strings and thongs, and the beast's flesh, as has been said, was a staple of the larder. The first great resolve of Ab and Oak, these two gallant soldiers of fortune, was that, alone and unaided, they would circumvent and slay one of these wild horses, thereby astonishing their respective families, at the same time gaining the means for filling the stomachs of those families to repletion, and altogether covering themselves with glory.

Not in a day nor in a week were the plans of these youthful warriors and statesmen matured. The wild horse had long since learned that the creature man was as dangerous to it as were any of the fierce four-footed animals which hunted it, and its scent was good and its pace was swift and it went in herds and avoided doubtful places. Not so easy a task as it might seem was that which Ab and Oak had resolved upon. There must be some elaborate device to attain their end, but they were confident. They had noted often what older hunters did, and they felt themselves as good as anybody. They plotted long and earnestly and even made a mental distribution of their quarry, deciding what should be done with its skin and with its meat, far in advance of any determination upon a plan for its capture and destruction. They were boys.

There was no objection from the parents. They knew that the boys must learn to become hunters, and if the two were not now capable of taking care of themselves in the wood, then they were but disappointing offspring. Consent secured, the boys acted entirely upon their own responsibility, and, to make their subsequent plans clearer, it may be well to explain a little more of the geography of the region. The cave of Ab was on the north side of the stream, where the rocky banks came close together with a little beach at either side, and the cave of Oak was perhaps a mile to the westward, on the same side of the stream and with very similar surroundings. On the south side of the river, opposite the high banks between the two caves, the land was a prairie valley reaching far away. On the north side as well there was at one place a little valley, but it reached back only a few hundred yards from the river and was surrounded by the forest-crowned hills. The close standing oaks and beeches afforded, in emergency, a highway among their branches, and along this pathway the boys were comparatively safe. Either could climb a tree at any time, and of the animals that were dangerous in the treetops there were but few; in fact, there was only one of note, a tawny, cat-like creature, not numerous, and resembling the lynx of the present day. Almost in the midst of the little plain or valley, on the north side of the river, rose a clump of trees, and in this the two boys saw means afforded them for a realization of their hopes. The wild horses fed daily in the valley to the north, as in the greater one to the south of the river. But there also, in the high grass, as upon the south, sometimes lurked the great beasts of prey, and to be far away from a tree upon the plain was an unsafe thing for a cave man. From the forest edge to the clump of trees was not more than two minutes' rush for a vigorous boy and it was this fact which suggested to the youths their plan of capture of the horse.

The homes of the cave men were located, when possible, where the refuge of safety overhung closely the river's bank, and where the non-climbing animals must pass along beneath them, but, even at that period of few men and abundant animal life, there had developed an acuteness among the weaker beasts, and they had learned to avoid certain paths that had proved fatal to their brethren. They were numerous in the plains and comparatively careless there, relying upon their speed to escape more dangerous wild beasts, but they passed rarely beneath the ledges, where a weighty rock dropped suddenly meant certain death. It was not a task entirely easy for the cave men to have meat with regularity, flush as was the life about them. New devices must be resorted to, and Ab and Oak were about to employ one not infrequently successful.

The clam of the period, particularly the clam along this reach of the upper Thames, was a marvel in his make-up. He was as large as he was luscious, as abundant as he was both and was a great feature in the food supply of the time. Not merely was he a feature in the food supply, but in a mechanical way, and the first object sought by the boys, after their plan had been agreed upon, was the shell of the great clam. They had no difficulty in securing what they wanted, for strewn all about each cave were the big shells in abundance. Sharp-edged, firm-backed, one of these shells made an admirable little shovel, something with which to cut the turf and throw up the soil, a most useful implement in the hands of the river haunting people. The idea of the youngsters was simply this: Their rendezvous should be at that point in the forest nearest the clump of trees standing solitary in the valley below. They would select the safest hours and then from the high ground make a sudden dash to the tree clump. They would be watchful, of course, and seek to avoid the class of animals for whom boys made admirable luncheon. Once at the clump of trees and safely ensconced among the branches, they could determine wisely upon the next step in their adventure. They were very knowing, these young men, for they had observed their elders. What they wanted to do, what was the end and aim of all this recklessness, was to dig a pit in this rich valley land close to the clump of trees, a pit say some ten feet in length by six feet in breadth and seven or eight feet in depth. That meant a gigantic labor. Gillian, of "The Toilers of the Sea," assigned to himself hardly a greater task. These were boys of the cave kind and must, perforce, conduct themselves originally. As to the details of the plan, well, they were only vague, as yet, but rapidly assuming a form more definite.

The first thing essential for the boys was to reach the clump of trees. It was just before noon one day when they swung together on a tree branch sweeping nearly to the ground, and at a point upon the hill directly opposite the clump. This was the time selected for their first dash. They studied every square yard of the long grass of the little valley with anxious eyes. In the distance was feeding a small drove of wild horses and, farther away, close by the river side, upreared occasionally what might be the antlers of the great elk of the period. Between the boys and the clump of trees there was no movement of the grass, nor any sign of life. They could discern no trace of any lurking beast.

"Are you afraid?" asked Ab.

"Not if we run together."

"All right," said Ab; "let's go it with a rush."

The slim brown bodies dropped lightly to the ground together, each of the boys clasping one of the clamshells. Side by side they darted down the slope and across through the deep grass until the clump of trees was reached,

when, like two young apes, they scrambled
into the safety of the branches.

The tree up which they had clambered was
the largest of the group and of dense foliage.
It was one of the huge conifers of the age, but
its branches extended to within perhaps thirty
feet of the ground, and from the greatest of
these side branches reached out, growing so
close together as to make almost a platform.
It was but the work of a half hour for these
boys, with their arboreal gifts, to twine addi-
tional limbs together and to construct for
themselves a solid nest and lookout where
they might rest at ease, at a distance above
the greatest leap of any beast existing. In
this nest they curled themselves down and,
after much clucking debate, formulated their
plan of operation. Only one boy should dig
at a time, the other must remain in the nest
as a lookout.

Swift to act in those days were men, because necessity had made it a habit to them,
and swifter still, as a matter of course, were
impulsive boys. Their tree nest fairly made,
work, they decided, must begin at once. The
only point to be determined upon was regarding the location of the pit. There was a

tempting spread of green herbage some hundred feet to the north and east of the tree, a place where the grass was high but not so high as it was elsewhere. It had been. grazed already by the wandering horses and it was likely that they would visit the tempting area again. There, it was finally settled, should the pit be dug. It was quite a distance from the tree, but the increased chances of securing a wild horse by making the pit in that particular place more than offset, in the estimation of the boys, the added danger of a longer run for safety in an emergency. The only question remaining was as to who should do the first digging and who be the first lookout? There was a violent debate upon this subject.

"I will go and dig and you shall keep watch," said Oak.

"No, I'll dig and you shall watch," was Ab's response. "I can run faster than you."

Oak hesitated and was reluctant. He was sturdy, this young gentleman, but Ab possessed, somehow, the mastering spirit. It was settled finally that Ab should dig and Oak should watch. And so Ab slid down the tree, clamshell in hand, and began laboring vigorously at the spot agreed upon.

It was not a difficult task for a strong boy to cut through tough grass roots with the keen edge of the clamshell. He outlined roughly and rapidly the boundaries of the pit to be dug and then began chopping out sods just as the workman preparing to garnish some park or lawn begins his work to-day. Meanwhile, Oak, all eyes, was peering in every direction. His place was one of great responsibility, and he recognized the fact. It was a tremendous moment for the youngsters.

CHAPTER VI.

A DANGEROUS VISITOR.

It was not alone necessary for the plans of
Ab and Oak that there should be made a deep
hole in the ground. It was quite as essential
for their purposes that the earth removed
should not be visible upon the adjacent surface. The location of the pit, as has been
explained, was some yards to the northeast
of the tree in which the lookout had been
made. A few yards southwest of the tree
was a slight declivity and damp hollow, for
from that point the land sloped in a reed-
grown marsh toward the river. It was decided to throw into this marsh all the exca-
vated soil, and so, when Ab had outlined the
pit and cut up its surface into sods, he carried
them one by one to the bank and cast them
down among the reeds where the water still
made little puddles. In time of flood the
river spread out into a lake, reaching even as
far as here. The sod removed, there was
exposed a rectangle of black soil, for the

earth was of alluvial deposit and easy of digging. Shellful after shellful of the dirt did Ab carry from where the pit was to be, trotting patiently back and forth, but the work was wearisome and there was a great waste of energy. It was Oak who gave an inspiration.

"We must carry more at a time," he called out. And then he tossed down to Ab a wolf-skin which had been given him by his father as a protection on cold nights and which he had brought along, tied about his waist, quite incidentally, for, ordinarily, these boys wore no clothing in warm weather. Clothing, in the cave time, appertained only to manhood and womanhood, save in winter. But Oak had brought the skin along because he had noticed a vast acorn crop upon his way to and from the rendezvous and had in mind to carry back to his own home cave some of the nuts. The pelt was now to serve an immediately useful purpose.

Spreading the skin upon the grass beside him, Ab heaped it with the dirt until there had accumulated as much as he could carry, when, gathering the corners together, he struggled with the enclosed load manfully to the bank and spilled it down into the morass. The digging went on rapidly until Ab, out of breath and tired, threw down the skin and climbed into the treetop and became the watchman, while Oak assumed his labor. So they worked alternately in treetop and upon the ground until the sun's rays shot red and slanting from the west. Wiser than to linger until dusk had too far deepened were these youngsters of the period. The clamshells were left in the pit. The lookout above declared nothing in sight, then slid to the ground and joined his friend, and another dash was made to the hill and the safety of its treetops. It was in great spirits that the boys separated to seek their respective homes. They felt that they were personages of consequence. They had no doubt of the success of the enterprise in which they had embarked, and the next day found them together again at an early hour, when the digging was enthusiastically resumed.

Many a load of dirt was carried on the second day from the pit to the marsh's edge, and only once did the lookout have occasion to suggest to his working companion that he had better climb the tree. A movement in the high grass some hundred yards away had aroused suspicion; some wild animal had passed, but, whatever it was, it did not approach the clump of trees and work was resumed at once. When dusk came the moist black soil found in the pit had all been carried away and the boys had reached, to their intense disgust, a stratum of hard packed gravel. That meant infinitely more difficult work for them and the use of some new utensil.

There was nothing daunting in the new problem. When it came to the mere matter of securing a tool for digging the hard gravel, both Ab and Oak were easily at home. The cave dwellers, haunting the river side for centuries, had learned how to deal with gravel, and when Ab returned to the scene the next day he brought with him a sturdy oaken stave some six feet in length, sharpened to a point and hardened in the fire until it was almost iron-like in its quality. Plunged into the gravel as far as the force of a blow could drive it, and pulled backward with the leverage obtained, the gravel was loosened and pried upward either in masses which could be lifted out entire, or so crumbled that it could be easily dished out with the clamshell. The work went on more slowly, but not less steadily nor hopefully than on the days preceding, and, for some time, was uninterrupted by any striking incident. The boys were becoming buoyant. They decided that the grassy valley was almost uninfested by things dangerous. They became reckless sometimes, and would work in the pit together. As a rule, though, they were cautious—this was an inherent and necessary quality of a cave being—and it was well for them that it was so, for when an emergency came only one of them was in the pit, while the other was aloft in the lookout and alert.

It was about three o'clock one afternoon when Ab, whose turn it chanced to be, was working valiantly in the pit, while Oak, all eyes, was perched aloft. Suddenly there came from the treetop a yell which was no boyish expression of exuberance of spirits. It was something which made Ab leap from the excavation as he heard it and reach the side of Oak as the latter came literally tumbling down the bole of the tree of watching.

"Run!" Oak said, and the two darted across the valley and reached the forest and clambered into safe hiding among the clus-

tering branches. Then, in the intervals between his gasping breath, Oak managed to
again articulate a word:

"Look!" he said.

Ab looked and, in an instant, realized how
wise had been Oak's alarming cry and how
well it was for them that they were so distant
from the clump of trees so near the river.
What he saw was that which would have
made the boys' fathers flee as swiftly had they
been in their children's place. Yet what Ab
looked upon was only a waving, in sinuous
regularity, of the rushes between the tree
clump and the river and the lifting of a head
some ten or fifteen feet above the reed-tops.
What had so alarmed the boys was what
would have disturbed a whole tribe of their
kinsmen, even though they had chanced to be
assembled, armed to the teeth with such
weapons as they then possessed. What they
saw was not of the common. Very rarely indeed, along the Thames, had occurred such an
invasion. The father of Oak had never seen
the thing at all, and the father of Ab had seen
it but once, and that many years before. It
was the great serpent of the seas!

Safely concealed in the branches of a tree

overlooking the little valley, the boys soon
recovered their normal breathing capacity and
were able to converse again. Not more than
a couple of minutes, at the utmost, had passed
between their departure from their place of
labor and their establishment in this same
tree. The creature which had so alarmed
them was still gliding swiftly across the morass
between the lowland and the river. It came
forward through the marsh undeviatingly toward the tree clump, the tall reeds quivering as
it passed, but its approach indicated by no
sound or other token of disturbance. The
slight bank reached, there was uplifted a great
serpent head, and then, without hesitation,
the monster swept forward to the trees and
soon hung dangling from the branches of the
largest one, its great coils twined loosely about
trunk and limb, its head swinging gently back
and forth just below the lower branch. It was
a serpent at least sixty feet in length, and two
feet or more in breadth at its huge middle. It
was queerly but not brilliantly spotted, and
its head was very nearly that of the anaconda
of to-day. Already the sea-serpent had become
amphibious. It had already acquired the knowledge it has transmitted to the anaconda, **that**

it might leave the stream, and, from some vantage point upon the shore, find more surely a victim than in the waters of the sea or river. This monster serpent was but waiting for the advent of any land animal, save perhaps those so great as the mammoth or the great elk, or, possibly, even the cave bear or the cave tiger. The mammoth was, of course, an impossibility, even to the sea-serpent. The elk, with its size and vast antlers, was, to put it at the mildest, a perplexing thing to swallow. The rhinoceros was dangerous, and as for the cave bear and the cave tiger, they were uncomfortable customers for anything alive. But there were the cattle, the aurochs and the urus, and the little horses and deer, and wild hog and a score of other creatures which, in the estimation of the sea-serpent, were extremely edible. A tidbit to the serpent was a man, but he did not get one in half a century.

Not long did the boys remain even in a harborage so distant. Each fled homeward with his story.

CHAPTER VII.

THE UNEXPECTED HAPPENS.

IT was with scant breath, when they reached their respective caves, that the boys told the story of the dread which had invaded the marsh-land. What they reported was no light event and, the next morning, their fathers were with them in the treetop at the safe distance which the wooded crest afforded and watching with apprehensive eyes the movements of the monster settled in the rugged valley tree. There was slight movement to note. Coiled easily around the bole, just above where the branches began, and resting a portion of its body upon a thick, extending limb, its head and perhaps ten or fifteen feet of its length swinging downward, the great serpent still hung awaiting its prey, ready to launch itself upon any hapless victim which might come within its reach. That its appetite would soon be gratified admitted of little doubt. Profiting by the absence of the boys, who while at work made no effort to conceal themselves, groups of wild horses were already feeding in the lowlands, and the elk and wild ox were visible here and there. The group in the treetop on the crest realized that it had business on hand. The sea-serpent was a terror to the cave people, and when one appeared to haunt the river the word was swiftly spread, and they gathered to accomplish its end if possible. With warnings to the boys they left behind them, the fathers sped away in different directions, one up, the other down, the river's bank, Stripe-Face to seek the help of some of the cave people and One-Ear to arouse the Shell people, as they were called, whose home was beside a creek some miles below. Into the home of the little colony One-Ear went swinging a little later, demanding to see the head man of the fishing village, and there ensued an earnest conversation of short sentences, but one which caused immediate commotion. To the hill dwellers the rare advent of a sea-serpent was comparatively a small matter, but it was a serious thing to the Shell folk. The sea-serpent might come up the creek and be among them at any moment, ravaging their community, The Shell people were grateful for the warning, but there were few of them at home, and less than a dozen could be mustered to go with One-Ear to the rendez-vous.

They were too late, the hardy people who came up to assail the serpent, because the serpent had not waited for them. The two boys roosting in the treetop on the height had beheld what was not pleasant to look upon, for they had seen a yearling of the aurochs enveloped by the thing, which whipped down suddenly from the branches, and the crushed quadruped had been swallowed in the serpent's way. But the dinner which might suffice it for weeks had not, in all entirety, the effect upon it which would follow the swallowing of a wild deer by its degenerate descendants of the Amazonian or Indian forests.

The serpent did not lie a listless mass, help-lessly digesting the product of the tragedy upon the spot of its occurrence, but crawled away slowly through the reeds, and instinct-ively to the water, into which it slid with scarce a splash, and then went drifting lazily away upon the current toward the sea. It had been years since one of these big water serpents had invaded the river at such a distance from its mouth and never came another up so far. There were causes promoting rapidly the extinction of their dreadful kind.

Three or four days were required before Ab and Oak realized, after what had taken place, that there were in the community any more important personages than they, and that they had work before them, if they were to continue in their glorious career. When every-day matters finally asserted themselves, there was their pit not yet completed. Because of their absence, a greater aggregation of beasts was feeding in the little valley. Not only the aurochs, the ancient bison, the urus, the progenitor of the horned cattle of to-day, wild horse and great elk and reindeer were seen within short distances from each other, but the big, hairy rhinoceros of the time was crossing the valley again and rioting in its herbage or wallowing in the pools where the valley dipped downward to the marsh. The mammoth with its young had swung clumsily across the area of rich feed, and, lurking in its train, eyeing hungrily and bloodthirstily the mammoth's calf, had crept the great cave tiger. The monster cave bear had shambled through the high grass, seeking some small food in default of that which might follow the conquest of a beast of size.   The uncomely hyenas had gone slinking here and there and had found something worthy their foul appetite.   All this change had come because the two boys, being boys and full of importance, had neglected their undertaking for about a week and had talked each in his own home with an air intended to be imposing, and had met each other with much dignity of bearing, at their favorite perching-place in the treetop on the hillside. When there came to them finally a consciousness that, to remain people of magnitude in the world, they must continue to do something, they went to work bravely.   The change which had come upon the valley in their brief absence tended to increase their confidence, for, as thus exhibited, early as was the age, the advent of the human being, young or old, somehow affected all animate nature and terrified it, and the boys saw this.   Not that the great beasts did not prey upon man, but then, as now, the man to the great beast was something of a terror, and man, weak as he was, knew himself and recognized himself as the head of all creation.   The mammoth, the huge, thick-coated rhinoceros, sabre-tooth, the monstrous tiger, or the bear, or the hyena, or the loping wolf, or short-bodied and vicious wolverine were to him, even then, but lower creatures. Man felt himself the master of the world, and his children inherited the perception.

Work in the pit progressed now rapidly and not a great number of days passed before it had attained the depth required. The boy at work was compelled, when emerging, to climb a dried branch which rested against the pit's edge, and the lookout in the tree exercised an extra caution, since his comrade below could no longer attain safety in a moment. But the work was done at last, that is, the work of digging, and there remained but the completion of the pitfall, a delicate though not a difficult matter. Across the pit, and very close together, were laid criss-crosses of slender branches, brought in armfuls from the forest; over these dry grass was spread, thinly but evenly, and over this again dust and dirt and more grass and twigs, all precautions being observed to give the place a natural appearance. In this the boys succeeded very well. Shrewd must have been the animal of any sort which could detect the trap. Their chief work done, the boys must now wait wisely. The place was deserted again and no nearer approach was made to the pitfall than the treetops of the hillside. There the boys were to be found every day, eager and anxious and hopeful as boys are generally. There was not occasion for getting closer to the trap, for, from their distant perch, its surface was distinctly visible and they could distinguish if it had been broken in. Those were days of suppressed excitement for the two; they could see the buffalo and wild horses moving here and there, but fortune was still perverse and the trap was not approached. Before its occupation by them, the place where they had dug had appeared the favorite feeding-place; now, with all perversity, the wild horses and other animals grazed elsewhere, and the boys began to fear that they had left some traces of their work which revealed it to the wily beasts. On one day, for an hour or two, their hearts were in their mouths. There issued from the forest to the westward the stately Irish elk. It moved forward across the valley to the waters on the other side, and, after drinking its fill, began feeding directly toward the tree clump. It reached the immediate vicinity of the pitfall and stood beneath the trees, fairly outlined against the opening beyond, and affording to the almost breathless couple a splendid spectacle. A magnificent creature was the great elk of the time of the cave men, the Irish elk, as those who study the past have named it, because its bones have been found so frequently in what are now the preserving peat bogs of Ireland. But the elk passed beyond the sight of the watchers, and so their bright hopes fell.

The crispness of full autumn had come, one morning, when Ab and Oak met as usual and looked out across the valley to learn if anything had happened in the vicinity of the pitfall. The hoar frost, lying heavily on the herbage, made the valley resemble a sea of silver, checkered and spotted all over darkly. These dark spots and lines were the traces of such animals as had been in the valley during the night or toward early morning. Leading everywhere were heavy trails and light ones, telling the story of the night. But very little heed to these things was paid by the ardent boys. They were too full of their own affairs. As they swung into place together upon their favorite limb and looked across the valley, they uttered a simultaneous and joyous shout. Something had taken place at the pitfall!

All about the trap the surface of the ground was dark and the area of darkness extended even to the little bank of the swamp on the riverside. Careless of danger, the boys dropped to the ground and, spears in hand, ran like deer toward the scene of their weeks of labor. Side by side they bounded to the edge of the excavation, which now yawned open to the sky. They had triumphed at last! As they saw what the pitfall held, they yelled in unison, and danced wildly around the opening, in the very height of boyish triumph. The exultation was fully justified, for the pitfall held a young rhinoceros, a creature only a few months old, but so huge already that it nearly filled the excavation. It was utterly helpless in the position it occupied. It was wedged in, incapable of moving more than slightly in any direction. Its long snout, with its sprouting pair of horns, was almost level with the surface of the ground and its small bright eyes leered wickedly at its noisy enemies. It struggled clumsily upon their approach, but nothing could relieve the hopelessness of its plight.

All about the pitfall the earth was plowed in furrows and beaten down by the feet of some monstrous animal. Evidently the calf was in the company of its mother when it fell a victim to the art of the pitfall diggers. It was plain that the mother had spent most of the night about her young in a vain effort to release it. Well did the cave boys understand the signs, and, after their first wild outburst of joy over the capture, a sense of the delicacy, not to say danger, of their situation came upon them. It was not well to interfere with the family affairs of the rhinoceros. Where had the mother gone? They looked about, but could see nothing to justify their fears. Only for a moment, though, did their sense of safety last; hardly had the echo of their shouting come back from the hillside than there was a splashing and rasping of bushes in the swamp and the rush of some huge animal toward the little ascent leading to the valley proper. There needed no word from either boy; the frightened couple bounded to the tree of refuge and had barely begun clambering up its trunk than there rose to view, mad with rage and charging viciously, the mother of the calf rhinoceros.

CHAPTER VIII.

SABRE-TOOTH AND RHINOCEROS.

THE rhinoceros of the Stone Age was a monstrous creature, an animal varying in many respects from either species of the animal of the present day, though perhaps somewhat closely allied to the huge double-horned and now nearly extinct white rhinoceros of southern Africa. But the brute of the prehistoric age was a beast of greater size, and its skin, instead of being bare, was densely covered with a dingy colored, crinkly hair, almost a wool. It was something to be dreaded by most creatures even in this time of great, fierce animals. It turned aside for nothing; it was the personification of courage and senseless ferocity when aroused. Rarely seeking a conflict, it avoided none. The hugh mammoth, a more peaceful pachyderm, would ordinarily hesitate before barring its path, while even the cave tiger, fiercest and most dreaded of the carnivora of the time, though it might prey upon the young rhinoceros when opportunity occurred, never voluntarily attacked the full-grown animal. From that almost impervious shield of leather hide, an inch or more in thickness, protected further by the woolly covering, even the terrible strokes of the tiger's claws glanced off with but a trifling rending, while one single lucky upward heave of the twin horns upon the great snout would pierce and rend, as if it were a trifling obstacle, the body of any animal existing. The lifting power of that prodigious neck was something almost beyond conception. It was an awful engine of death when its opportunity chanced to come. On the other hand, the rhinoceros of this ancient world had but a limited range of vision, and was as dull-witted and dangerously impulsive as its African prototype of to-day.

But short-sighted as it was, the boys clambering up the tree were near enough for the perception of the great beast which burst over the hummock, and it charged directly at them, the tree quivering when the shoulder of the monster struck it as it passed, though the boys, already in the branches, were in safety. Checking herself a little distance beyond, the rhinoceros mother returned, snorting fiercely, and began walking round and round the calf imprisoned in the pitfall.   The boys comprehended perfectly the story of the night.   The calf once ensnared, the mother had sought in vain to rescue it, and, finally, wearied with her exertion, had retired just over the little descent, there to wallow and rest while still keeping guard over her imprisoned young. The spectacle now, as she walked around the trap, was something which would have been pitiful to a later race of man.   The beast would get down upon her knees and plow the dirt about the calf with her long horns. She would seek to get her snout beneath its body sidewise, and so lift it, though each effort was necessarily futile.   There was no room for any leverage, the calf fitted the cavity.   The boys clung to their perches in safety, but in perplexity.   Hours passed, but the mother rhinoceros showed no inclination to depart.   It was three o'clock in the afternoon when she went away to the wallow, returning once or twice to her young before descending the bank, and, even when she had reached the marsh, snorting querulously for some time before settling down to rest.

The boys waited until all was quiet in the

marsh, and, as a matter of prudence, for some time longer. They wanted to feel assured that the monster was asleep, then, quietly, they slid down the tree trunk and, with noiseless step, stole by the pitfall and toward the hillside. A few yards further on their pace changed to a run, which did not cease until they reached the forest and its refuge, nor, even there, did they linger for any length of time. Each started for his home; for their adventure had again assumed a quality which demanded the consideration of older heads and the assistance of older hands. It was agreed that they should again bring their fathers with them—by a fortunate coincidence each knew where to find his parent on this particular day—and that they should meet as soon as possible. It was more than an hour later when the two fathers and two sons, the men armed with the best weapons they possessed, appeared upon the scene.

So far as the watchers from the hillside could determine, all was quiet about the clump of trees and the vicinity of the pitfall. It was late in the afternoon now and the men decided that the best course to pursue would be to steal down across the valley, kill the imprisoned calf and then escape as soon as possible, leaving the mother to find her offspring dead; reasoning that she would then abandon it. Afterward the calf could be taken out and there would be a feast of cave men upon the tender food and much benefit derived in utilization of the tough yet not, at its age, too thick hide of the uncommon quarry.   There was but one difficulty in the way of carrying out this enterprise: the wind was from the north and blew from the hunters toward the river, and the rhinoceros, though lacking much range of vision, was as acute of scent as the gray wolves which sometimes strayed like shadows through the forest or the hyenas which scented from afar the living or the dead.   Still, the venture was determined upon.

The four descended the hill, the two boys in the rear, treading with the lightness of the tiger cat, and went cautiously across the valley and toward the tree trunk.   Certainly no sound they made could have reached the ear of the monster wallowing below the bank, but the wind carried to its nostrils the message of their coming.   They were not half way across the valley when the rhinoceros floundered up to

the level and charged wildly along the course
of the wafted scent. There was a flight for
the hillside, made none too soon, but yet in
time for safety. Walking around in circles,
snorting viciously, the great beast lingered in
the vicinity for a time, then went back to its
imprisoned calf, where it repeated the performance of earlier in the day and finally retired again to its hidden resting-place near by.
It was dusk now and the shadows were deepening about the valley.

The men, well up in the tree with the
boys, were undetermined what to do. They
might steal along to the eastward and approach
the calf from another direction without disturbing the great brute by their scent. But
it was becoming darker every moment and the
region was a dangerous one. In the valley
and away from the trees they were at a disadvantage and at night there were fearful things
abroad. Still, they decided to take the risk,
and the four, following the crest of the slight
hill, moved along its circle southeastward
toward the river bank, each on the alert and
each with watchful eyes scanning the forest
depths to the left or the valley to the right. Suddenly One-Ear leaped back into the shadow,

waved his hand to check the advance of those
behind him, then pointed silently across the
valley and toward the clump of trees.

Not a hundred yards from the pitfall the
high grass was swaying gently; some creature
was passing along toward the pitfall and a
thing of no slight size.   Every eye of the quar-
tet was strained now to learn what might be
the interloper upon the scene.   It was nearly
dark, but the eyes of the cave men, almost
nocturnal in their adaptation as they were,
distinguished a long, dark body emerging from
the reeds and circling curiously and cautiously
around the pitfall; nearer and nearer it approached the helpless prisoner until perhaps
twenty feet distant from it.   Here the thing
seemed to crouch and remain quiescent, but
only for a little time.   Then resounded across
the valley a screaming roar, so fierce and rau-
cous and death-telling and terrifying that even
the hardened hunters leaped with affright.   At
the same moment a dark object shot through
the air and landed on the back of the creature
in the shallow pit.   The tiger was abroad!
There was a wild bleat of terror and agony, a
growl fiercer and shorter than the first hoarse
cry of the tiger, and, then, for a moment silence,

but only for a moment. Snorts, almost as terrible in their significance as the tiger's roar, came from the marsh's edge. A vast form loomed above the slight embankment and there came the thunder of ponderous feet. The rhinoceros mother was charging the great tiger!

There was a repetition of the fierce snorts, with the wild rush of the rhinoceros, another roar, the sound of which reëchoed through the valley, and then could be dimly seen a black something flying through the air and alighting, apparently, upon the back of the charging monster. There was a confusion of forms and a confusion of terrifying sounds, the snarling roar of the great tiger and half whistling bellow of the great pachyderm, but nothing could be seen distinctly. That a gigantic duel was in progress the cave men knew, and knew, as well, that its scene was one upon which they could not venture. The clamor had not ended when the darkness became complete and then each father, with his son, fled swiftly homeward.

Early the next morning, the four were together again at the same point of safety and advantage, and again the frost-covered valley was a sea of silver, this time unmarred by the criss-crosses of feeding or hunting animals. There was no sign of life; no creature of the forest or the plain was so daring as to venture soon upon the battlefield of the rhinoceros and the cave tiger. Cautiously the cave men and their sons made their way across the valley and approached the·pitfall. What was revealed to them told in a moment the whole story. The half-devoured body of the rhinoceros calf was in the pit. It had been killed, no doubt, by the tiger's first fierce assault, its back broken by the first blow of the great forearm, or its vertebræ torn apart by the first grasp of the great jaws. There were signs of the conflict all about, but that it had not come to a deadly issue was apparent. Only by some accident could the rhinoceros have caught upon its horns the agile monster cat, and only by an accident even more remote could the tiger have reached a vital part of its huge enemy. There had been a long and weary battle—a mother creature fighting for her young and the great flesh-eater fighting for his prey. But the combatants had assuredly separated without the death of either, and the bereaved rhinoceros, knowing her young one to be dead, had finally left the valley, while

the tiger had returned to its prey and fed its
fill. But there was much meat left. There
were, in the estimation of the cave people,
few more acceptable feasts than that obtain-
able from the flesh of a young rhinoceros.
The first instinct of the two men was to work
fiercely with their flint knives and cut out
great lumps of meat from the body in the pit.
Hardly had they begun their work, when, as
by common impulse, each clambered out from
the depression suddenly, and there was a brief
and earnest discussion. The cave tiger, mon-
arch of the time, was not a creature to abandon what he had slain until he had devoured
it utterly. Gorged though he might be, he
was undoubtedly in hiding within a comparatively short distance. He would return again
inevitably. He might be lying sleeping in
the nearest clump of bushes! It was possible
that his appetite might come upon him soon
again and that he might appear at any moment. What chance then for the human
beings who had ventured into his dining-room?
There was but one sensible course to follow,
and that was instant retreat. The four fled
again to the hillside and the forest, carrying
with them, however, the masses of flesh al-

ready severed from the body of the calf.
There was food for a day or two for each
family.

And so ended the first woodland venture of
these daring boys.   For days the vicinity of
the little valley was not sought by either man
or youth, since the tiger might still be lurking
near.   When, later, the youths dared to visit
the scene of their bold exploit, there were
only bones in the pitfall they had made.   The
tiger had eaten its prey and had gone to other
fields.   In later autumn came a great flood
down the valley, rising so high that the father
of Oak and all his family were driven temporarily from their cave by the water's influx
and compelled to seek another habitation
many miles away.   Some time passed before
the comrades met again.

As for Ab, this exploit might be counted
almost as the beginning of his manhood.   His
father—and fathers had even then a certain
paternal pride—had come to recognize in a
degree the vigor and daring of his son.
The mother, of course, was even more appre-
ciative, though to her firstborn she could give
scant attention, as Ab had the small brother
in the cave now and the little sister who was

stil. smaller, but from this time the youth became a person of some importance. He grew
rapidly, and the sinewy stripling developed,
not increasing strength and stature and rounding brawn alone, for he had both ingenuity
and persistency of purpose, qualities which
made him rather an exception among the cave
boys of his age.

CHAPTER IX.

DOMESTIC MATTERS.

ATTENTION has already been called to the fact that the family of Ab were of the aristocracy of the region, and it should be added that the interior of One-Ear's mansion corresponded with his standing in the community. It was a fine cave, there was no doubt about that, and Red-Spot was a notable housekeeper. As a rule, the bones remaining about the fire after a meal were soon thrown outside—at least they were never allowed to accumulate for more than a month or two. The beds were excellent, for, in addition to the mass of leaves heaped upon the earth which formed a resting-place for the family, there were spread the skins of various animals. The water privileges of the establishment were extensive, for there was the river in front, much utilized—for drinking purposes. There were ledges and shelves of rock projecting here and there from the sides of the cave, and upon these were laid the weapons and implements of the household,

so that, excepting an occasional bone upon
the earthen floor, or, perhaps, a spattering of
red, where some animal had been cut up for
roasting, the place was very neat indeed. The
fact that the smoke from the fire could, when
the wind was right, ascend easily through the
roof made the residence one of the finest within
a large district of the country. As to light, it
cannot be said that the house was well pro-
vided. The fire at night illuminated a small
area and, in the daytime, light entered through
the doorway, and, to an extent, through the
hole in the cave's top, as did also the rains,
but the light was by no means perfect. The
doorway, for obvious reasons, was narrow and
there was a huge rock, long ago rolled inside
with much travail, which could on occasion be
utilized in blocking the narrow passage.
Barely room to squeeze by this obstruction
existed at the doorway. The sneaking but
dangerous hyena had a keen scent and was
full of curiosity. The monster bear of the time
was ever hungry and the great cave tiger,
though rarer, was, as has been shown, a haunting dread. Great attention was paid to door-
ways in those days, not from an artistic point
of view exactly, but from reasons cogent enough

in the estimation of the cave men. But the cave was warm and safe and the sharp eyes of its inhabitants, accustomed to the semi-darkness, found slight difficulty in discerning objects in the gloom. Very content with their habitation were all the family and Red-Spot particularly, as a chatelaine should, felt much pride in her surroundings.

It may be added that the family of One-Ear was a happy one. His life with Red-Spot was the sequence of what might be termed a fortunate marriage. It is true that standards vary with times, and that the demeanor of the couple toward each other was occasionally not what would be counted the index of domestic felicity in this more artificial and deceptive age. It was never fully determined whether One-Ear or Red-Spot could throw a stone ax with the greater accuracy, although certainly he could hurl one with greater force than could his wife. But the deftness of each in eluding such dangerous missiles was about the same, and no great harm had at any time resulted from the effects of momentary ebullitions of anger, followed by action on the part of either. There had not been at any time a scandal in the family. The pair were faithful to each other. Society was somewhat scattered in those days, and the cave twain, anywhere, were generally as steadfast as the lion and the lioness. It was centuries later, too, before the cave men's posterity became degenerate enough or prosperous enough, or safe enough, to be polygamous, and, so far as the area of the Thames valley or even the entire "Paris basin," as it is called, was concerned, monogamy held its own very fairly, from the shell-beds of the earliest kitchen-middens to the time of the bronze ax and the dawn of what we now call civilization.

There were now five members in this family of the period, One-Ear, Red-Spot, Ab, Bark and Beech-Leaf, the two last named being Ab's younger brother and little more than baby sister. The names given them had come in the same accidental way as had the name of Ab. The brother, when very small, had imitated in babyish way the barking of some wolfish creature outside which had haunted the cave's vicinity at night time, and so the name of Bark, bestowed accidentally by Ab himself, had become the youngster's title for life. As to Beech-Leaf, she had gained her name in another way. She was a fat and joyous little specimen of a cave baby and not much addicted to lying as dormant as babies sometimes do. The bearskin upon which her mother laid her had not infrequently proven too limited an area for her exploits and she would roll from it into the great bed of beech leaves upon which it was placed, and become fairly lost in the brown mass. So often had this hilarious young lady to be disinterred from the beech leaf bed, that the name given her came naturally, through association of ideas. Between the birth of Ab and that of his younger brother an interval of five years had taken place, the birth of the sister occurring three or four years later. So it came that Ab, in the absence of his father and mother, was distinctly the head of the family, admonitory to his brother, with ideas as to the physical discipline requisite on occasion, and, in a rude way, fond of and protective toward the baby sister.

There was a certain regularity in the daily program of the household, although, with reference to what was liable to occur outside, it can hardly be said to have partaken of the element of monotony. The work of the day consisted merely in getting something to eat, and in this work father and mother alike took an active part, their individual duties being somewhat varied. In a general way One-Ear relied upon himself for the provision of flesh, but there were roots and nuts and fruits, in their season, and in the gathering of these Red-Spot was an admitted expert. Not that all her efforts were confined to the fruits of the soil and forest, for she could, if need be, assist her husband in the pursuit or capture of any animal. She was not less clever than he in that animal's subsequent dissection, and was far more expert in its cooking. In the tanning of skins she was an adept. So it chanced that at this time the father and mother frequently left the cave together in the morning, their elder son remaining as protector of the younger inmates. When occasionally he went with his parents, or was allowed to venture forth alone, extra precautions were taken as to the cave's approaches. Just outside the entrance was a stone similar to the one on the inside, and when the two young children were left unguarded this outside barricade was rolled against what remained of the entrance, so that the small people, though prisoners, were at least secure from dangerous amimals. Of course there were variations in the program

There was that degree of fellowship among
the cave men, even at this early age, to allow
of an occasional banding together for hunting
purposes, a battle of some sort or the surrounding and destruction of some of the
greater animals. At such times One-Ear
would be absent from the cave for days and
Ab and his mother would remain sole guardians. The boy enjoyed these occasions im-
mensely; they gave him a fine sense of responsibility and importance, and did much
toward the development of the manhood that
was in him, increasing his self-reliance and
perfecting him in the art of winning his daily
bread, or what was daily bread's equivalent
at the time in which he lived. It was not in
outdoor and physical life alone that he grew.
There was something more to him, a combination of traits somewhere which made him a
little beyond and above the mere seeker after
food. He was never entirely dormant, a
sleeper on the skins and beech leaves, even
when in the shelter of the cave, after the
day's adventures. He reasoned according to
such gifts as circumstances had afforded him
and he had the instinct of devising. An instinct toward devising was a great thing to its
possessor in the time of the cave people.

We know very well to-day, of think we know, that the influence of the mother, in most cases, dominates that of the father in making the future of the man-child. It may be that this comes because in early life the boy, throughout the time when all he sees or learns will be most clear in his memory until he dies, is more with the woman parent than with the man, who is afield; or, it may be, there is some criss-cross law of nature which makes the man ordinarily transmit his qualities to the daughter and the woman transmit hers to the son. About that we do not know yet. But it is certain that Ab was more like his mother than his father, and that in these young days of his he was more immediately under her influence. And Red-Spot was superior in many ways to the ordinary woman of the cave time.

It was good for the boy that he was so under the maternal dominion, and that, as he lingered about the cave, he aided in the making of threads of sinew or intestine, or looked on interestedly as his mother, using the bone needle, which he often sharpened for her with his flint scraper, sewed together the skins which made the garments of the family. The needle was one without an eye, a mere awl, which made holes through which the thread was pushed. As the growing boy lounged or labored near his mother, alternately helpful or annoying, as the case might be, he learned many things which were of value to him in the future, and resolved upon brave actions which should be greatly to his credit. He was but a cub, a young being almost as un-reasoning in some ways as the beasts of the wood, but he had his hopes and vanities, as has even the working beaver or the dancing crane, and from the long mother-talks came a degree of definiteness of outline to his ambitions. He would be the greatest hunter and warrior in all the region!

The cave mother easily understood her child's increasing daringness and vigor, and though swift to anger and strong of hand, she could not but feel a pride in and tell her tales to the boy beside her. After a time, when the family of Oak returned to the cave above and the boys were much together again, the mother began to see less of her son. The influence of the days spent by her side remained with the boy, however, and much that he learned there was of value in his later active life.

CHAPTER X.

OLD MOK, THE MENTOR.

IT was at about this time, the time when Ab had begun to develop from boyhood into strong and aspiring youth, that his family was increased from five to six by the addition of a singular character, Old Mok. This personage was bent and seemingly old, but he was younger than he looked, though he was not extremely fair to look upon. He had a shock of grizzled hair, a short, stiff, unpleasant beard, and the condition of one of his legs made him a cripple of an exaggerated type. He could hobble about and on great occasions make a journey of some length, but he was practically debarred from hunting. The extraordinary curvature of his twisted leg was, as usual in his time, the result of an encounter with some wild beast. The limb curved like a corkscrew and was so much shorter than the other leg that the man was really safe only when the walls of a cave enclosed him. But if his legs were weak his brain and arms were not. In that grizzled head was much intelligence and the arms were those of a great climber. His toes were clasping things and he was at home in a treetop. But he did not travel much. There was no need.

Old Mok had special gifts, and they were such as made him a desirable friend among the cave men. He had, in his youth, been a mighty hunter and had so learned that he could tell wonderfully the ways of beasts and swimming things and the ways of slaying or eluding them. Best of all, he was such a fashioner of weapons as the valley had rarely known, and, because of this, was in great request as a cared-for inmate of almost any cave which hit his fancy. After his crippling he had drifted from one haven to another, never quite satisfied with what he found, and now he had come to live, as he supposed, with his old friend, One-Ear, until life should end. Despite his harshness of appearance—and neither of the two could ever afterward explain it—there was something about the grim old man which commended him to Ab from the very first. There was an occasional twinkle in the fierce old fellow's eye and sometimes a certain cackle in his clucking talk, which betokened not unkindliness toward a healthy youngster, and the two soon grew together, as often the young and old may do.

Though but what might be called in one sense a dependent, the crippled hunter had a dignity and was arbitrary in the expression of his views. Never once, through all the thousands of years which have passed since he hobbled here and there, has lived an armorer more famous among those who knew him best. No fashioner of sword, or lance, or coat of mail or plate, in the far later centuries, had better reputation than had Mok with his friends and patrons for the making of good weapons, though it may be that his clientele was less numerous by hundreds to one than that of some later manufacturer of a Toledo blade. He might be living partly as a dependent, but he could do almost as he willed. Who should have standing if it were not accorded to the most gifted chipper of flint and carver of mammoth tooth in all the region from where the little waters came down to make a river, to where the blue, broad stream, blending with friendly currents, was lost in what is now the great North Sea?

A boy and an old man can come together

closely, and that has, through all the ages, been a good thing for each. The boy learns that which enables him to do things and the man is happy in watching the development of one of his own kind. Helping and advising Ab, and sometimes Oak as well, Old Mok did not discourage sometimes reckless undertakings. In those days chances were accepted. So when any magnificient scheme suggested itself to the two youths, Ab at once sought his adviser and was not discountenanced.

It was a great night in the cave when Ab brought home two fluffy gray bundles not much larger than kittens and tied them in a corner with thongs of sinew, sinew so tough and stringy that it could not easily be severed by the sharp teeth which were at once applied to it. The fluffy gray bundles were two young wolves, and were, for Ab, a great possession. They were not even brother and sister, these cubs, and had been gallantly captured by the two courageous rangers, Ab and Oak. For some time the boys had noted lurking shadows about a rugged height close by the river, some distance below the cave of Ab, and had resolved upon a closer investigation. A particularly ugly brute was the wolf of the cave man's time, but one which, when not in pack, was unlikely to assail two well-armed and sturdy youths in daylight; and the result of much cautious spying was that they found two dens, each with young in them, and at a time when the old wolves were away. In one den Ab seized upon two of the snarling cubs and Oak did the same in the other, and then the raiders fled with such speed as was in them, until they were at a safe distance from the place where things would not go well with them should the robbed parents return. Once in safe territory, each exchanged a cub for one seized by the other and then each went home in triumph. Ab was especially delighted. He was determined to feed his cubs with the utmost care and to keep them alive and growing. He was full of the fancy and delighted in it, but he had assumed a great responsibility.

The cubs were tied in a corner of the cave and at once commanded the attention and unbounded admiration of Bark and Beechleaf. The young lady especially delighted in the little beasts and could usually be found lying in the corner with them, the baby wolves learning in time to play with her as if she

were a wolf-suckled cub herself. Bark had
almost the same relations with the little brutes
and Ab looked after them most carefully.
Even the father and mother became interested
in the antics of the young children and young
wolves and the cubs became acknowledged,
if not particularly respected, members of the
family. But Ab's dream was too much for
sudden realization. Not all at once could the
wild thing become a tame one. As the cubs
grew and their teeth became longer and
sharper, there was an occasional conflict and
the arms of Bark and Beechleaf were scarred
in consequence, until at last Ab, though he
protested hardly, was compelled to give up
his pets. Somehow, he was not in the mood
for killing the half grown beasts, and so he
simply turned them loose, but they did not,
as he had thought they would, flee to the forest. They had known almost no life except
that of the cave, they had got their meat there
and, at night, the twain were at the doorway
whining for food. To tnem were tossed some
half-gnawed bones and they received them
with joyous yelps and snarls. Thenceforth
they hung about the cave and retained, practically, their place in the family, oddly enough

showing particular animosity to those of their own kind who ventured near the place. One day, the female was found in the cave's rear with four little whelps lying beside her, and that settled it! The family petted the young animals and they grew up tamer and more obedient than had been their father and mother. Protected by man, they were unlikely to revert to wildness. Members of the pack which grew from them were, in time, bestowed as valued gifts among the cave men of the region and much came of it. The two boys did a greater day's work than they could comprehend when they raided the dens by the river's side.

But there was much beside the capture of wolf cubs to occupy the attention of the boys. They counted themselves the finest bird hunters in the community and, to a certain extent, justified the proud claim made. No youths could set a snare more deftly or hurl a stone more surely, and there was much bird life for them to seek. The bustard fed in the vast nut forests, the capercailzie was proud upon the moors, where the heath-cock was as jaunty, and the willow grouse and partridge were wise in covert to avoid the hungry snowy owl. Upon the river and lagoons and creeks the swan and wild goose and countless duck made constant clamor, and there were water-rail and snipe along the shallows. There were eggs to be found, and an egg baked in the ashes was a thing most excellent. It was with the waterfowl that the boys were most successful. The ducks would in their feeding approach close to the shores of the river banks or the little islands and would gather in bunches so near to where the boys were hidden that the young hunters, leaping suddenly to their feet and hurling their stones together, rarely failed to secure at least a single victim. There were muskrats along the banks and there was a great beaver, which was not abundant, and which was a mighty creature of his kind. Of muskrats the boys speared many—and roasted muskrat is so good that it is eaten by the Indians and some of the white hunters in Canada to-day—but the big beaver they did not succeed in capturing at this stage of their career. Once they saw a seal, which had come up the river from the sea, and pursued it, running along the banks for miles, but it proved as elusive as the great beaver.

But, as a matter of course, it was upon land that the greatest sport was had. There were the wild hogs, but the hogs were wary and the big boars dangerous, and it was only when a litter of the young could be pounced upon somewhere that flint-headed spears were fully up to the emergency. On such occasions there was fine pigsticking, and then the atmosphere in the caves would be made fascinating with the odor of roasting suckling. There is a story by a great and gentle writer telling how a Chinaman first discovered the beauties of roast pig. It is an admirable tale and it is well that it was written, but the cave man, many tens of thousands of years before there was a China, yielded to the allurements of young pig, and sought him accordingly.

The musk-ox, which still mingled with the animals of the river basin, was almost as difficult of approach as in arctic wilds to-day, as was a small animal, half goat, half antelope, which fed upon the rocky hillsides or wherever the high reaches were. There were squirrels in the trees, but they were seldom caught, and the tailless hare which fed in the river meadows was not easily approached and was swift as the sea wind in its flight, swifter than a

sort of fox which sought it constantly.   But
the burrowing things were surer game.   There
were martens and zerboas, and marmots and
hedgehogs and badgers, all good to eat and
attainable to those who could dig as could
these brawny youths.   The game once driven
to its hole, the clamshell and the sharpened
fire-hardened spade-stick were brought into
use and the fate of the animal sought was
rarely long in doubt.   It is true that the scene
lacked one element very noticeable when boys
dig out any animal to-day.   There was not
the inevitable and important dog, but the
youths were swift of sight and quick of hand,
and the hidden creature, once unearthed, seldom escaped.   One of the prizes of those
feats of excavation was the badger, for not
only was it edible, but its snow-white teeth,
perforated and strung on sinew, made neck-
laces which were highly valued.

The youths did not think of attacking many
of the dangerous brutes.   They might have
risked the issue with a small leopard which
existed then, or faced the wildcat, but what
they sought most was the wolverine, because
it had fur so long and oddly marked, and because it was braver than other animals of its

size and came more boldly to some bait of
meat, affording opportunity for fine spear-
throwing. And, apropos of the wolverine,
the glutton, as it is called in Europe, it is
something still admired. It is a vicious,
bloodthirsty, unchanging and, to the widely-in-
formed and scientifically sentimental, lovable
animal. It is vicious and bloodthirsty because that is its nature. It is lovable because,
through all the generations, it has come down
just the same. The cave man knew it just as
it is now; the early Teuton knew it when
"hides" of land were the rewards of warriors.
The Roman knew it when he made forays to
the far north for a few centuries and learned
how sharp were the blades of the Rhine-folk
and the Briton. The Druid and the Angle and
Jute and Saxon knew it, and it is known to-day
in all northern Europe and Asia and America,
in fact, in nearly all the northern temperate
zone. The wolverine is something wonderful;
it laughs at the ages; its bones, found side by
side with those of the cave hyena, are the
same as those found in its body as it exists to-
day. It is an anomaly, an animal which does
not advance nor retrograde.

The two big boys grew daily in the science

of gaining food and grew more and more of importance in their respective households. Sometimes either one of them might hunt alone, but this was not the rule. It was safer for two than one, when the forest was invaded deeply. But not all their time was spent in evading or seeking the life of such living things as they might discover. They had a home life sometimes as entertaining as the life found anywhere outside.

CHAPTER XI.

THOSE were happy times in the cave, where Ab, developing now into an exceedingly stalwart youth, found the long evenings about the fire far from monotonous. There was Mok, the mentor, who had grown so fond of him, and there was most interesting work to do in making from the dark flint nodules or obsidian fragments—always eagerly seized upon when discovered by the cave people in their wanderings—the spearheads and rude knives and skin scrapers so essential to their needs. The flint nodule was but a small mass of the stone, often somewhat pear-shaped. Though apparently a solid mass, composed of the hardest substance then known, it lay in what might be called a series of flakes about a center, and, in wise hands, these flakes could be chipped or pried away unbroken. The flake, once won, was often slightly concave on the outside and convex on the other, but the core of the stone was something more equally balanced in for-

mation and, when properly finished, made a
mighty spearhead.   For the heavy axes and
mallets, other stones, such as we now call
granite, redstone or quartose grit, were often
used, but in the making of all the weapons
was required the exercise of infinite skill and
patience.   To make the flakes symmetrical
demanded the nicest perception and judgment
of power of stroke, for, with each flake gained,
there resulted a new form to the surface of the
stone.   The object was always to secure a
flake with a point, a strong middle ridge and
sides as nearly edged as possible.   And in the
striking off of these flakes and their finishing
others of the cave men were to old Mok as
the child is to the man.

Ab hung about the old man at his work and
was finally allowed to help him.   If, at first,
the boy could do nothing else, he could, with
his flint scraper, work industriously at the
smoothing of the long spear shafts, and when
he had learned to do well at this he was at last
allowed to venture upon the stone chipping,
especially when into old Mok's possession had
come a piece of flint the quality of which he
did not quite approve and for the ruining of
which in the splitting he cared but little.

There were disasters innumerable when the
boy began and much bad stone was spoiled,
but he had a will and a good eye and hand,
and it came, in time, that he could strike off a
flake with only a little less of deftness than his
teacher and that, even in the more delicate
work of the finer chipping to complete the
weapon, he was a workman not to be despised.
He had an ambition in it all and old Mok was
satisfied with what he did.

The boy was always experimenting, ever
trying a new flint chipper or using a third stone
to tap delicately the one held in the hand to
make the fracture, or wondering aloud why it
would not be well to make this flint knife a
little thinner, or that spearhead a trifle heavier.
He was questioning as he worked and something of a nuisance with it all, but old Mok
endured with what was, for him, an astonishing degree of patience, and would sometimes
comment grumblingly to the effect that the
boy could at least chip stone far better than
some men.   And then the veteran would look
at One-Ear, who was, notoriously, a bad flint
worker,—though, a weapon once in his grasp,
there were few could use it with surer eye or
heavier hand—and would chuckle as he made

the comment. As for One-Ear, he listened
placidly enough. He was glad a son of his
could make good weapons. So much the
better for the family!

As times went, Ab was a tolerably good boy
to his mother. Nearly all young cave males
were good boys until the time came when their
thews and sinews outmatched the strength of
those who had borne them, and this, be it said,
was at no early age, for the woman, hunting
and working with the man, was no maternal
weakling whose buffet was unworthy of notice.
A blow from the cave mother's hand was something to be respected and avoided. The use
of strength was the general law, and the cave
woman, though she would die for her young,
yet demanded that her young should obey her
until the time came when the maternal instinct
of first direction blended with and was finally
lost in pride over the force of the being to
whom she had given birth. So Ab had vigorous duties about the household.

As has been told already, Red-Spot was a
notable housekeeper and there was such product of the cave cooking as would make happy
any gourmand of to-day who could appreciate
the quality of what had a most natural flavor.

Regarding her kitchen appliances Red-Spot had a matron's justifiable pride. Not only was there the wood fire, into which, held on long, pointed sticks, could be thrust all sorts of meat for the somewhat smoky broiling, and the hot coals and ashes in which could be roasted the clams and the clay-covered fish, but there was the place for boiling, which only the more fortunate of the cave people owned. Her growing son had aided much in the attainment of this good housewife's fond desire.

With much travail, involving all the force the cave family could muster and including the assistance of Oak's father and of Oak himself, who rejoiced with Ab in the proceedings, there had been rolled into the cave a huge sandstone rock with a top which was nearly flat. Here was to be the great pot, sometimes used as a roasting place, as well, which only the more pretentious of the caves could boast. On the middle of the big stone's uppermost surface old Mok chipped with an ax the outline of a rude circle some two feet in diameter. This defined roughly the size of the kettle to be made. Inside the circle, the sandstone must be dug out to a big kettle's proper depth, and upon

the boy, Ab, must devolve most of this health-
ful but not over-attractive labor.

The boy went at the task gallantly, in the
beginning, and pecked away with a stone
chisel and gained a most respectable hollow
within a day or two, but his enthusiasm sub-
sided with the continuity of much effort with
small result. He wanted more weight to his
chisel of flint set firmly in reindeer's horn, and
a greater impact to the blows into which could
not be put the force resulting from a swing of
arm. He thought much. Then he secured a
long stick and bound his chisel strongly to it at
one end, the top of the chisel resting against a
projecting stub of limb, so that it could not be
driven upward. To the other end of the stick
he bound a stone of some pounds in weight
and then, holding the shaft with both hands,
lifted it and let the whole drop into the depression he had already made. The flint chisel
bit deeply under the heavy impact and the
days were few before Ab had dug in the sandstone rock a cavity which would hold much
meat and water. There was an unconscious
celebration when the big kettle was completed.
It was nearly filled with water, and into the
water were flung great chunks of the meat of a

reindeer killed that day. Meanwhile, the cave fire had been replenished with dry wood and there had been formed a wide bed of coals, upon which were cast numerous stones of moderate size, which soon attained a shining heat. A sort of tongs made of green withes served to remove the stones, one after another, from the mass of coal, and drop them in with the meat and water. Within a little time the water was fairly boiling and soon there was a monster stew giving forth rich odors and ready to be eaten. And it was not allowed to get over-cool after that summoning fragrance had once extended throughout the cave. There was a rush for the clam shells which served for soup dishes or cups, there was spearing with sharpened sticks for pieces of the boiled meat, and all were satisfied, though there was shrill complaint from Bark, whose turn at the kettle came late, and much clamor from chubby Beech-leaf, who was not yet tall enough to help herself, but who was cared for by the mother. It may be that, to some people of to-day, the stew would be counted lacking in quality of seasoning, but an opinion upon seasoning depends largely upon the stomach and the time, and, besides, it may be that the dirt clinging to the stones cast into the water gave a certain flavor as fine in its way as could be imparted by salt and pepper.

Old Mok, observing silently, had decidedly approved of Ab's device for easier digging into sandstone than was the old manner of pecking away with a chisel held in the hand. He was almost disposed now to admit the big lad to something like a plane of equality in the work they did together. He became more affable in their converse, and the youth was, in the same degree, delighted and ambitious, They experimented with the stick and weight and chisel in accomplishing the difficult work of splitting from boulders the larger fragments of stone from which weapons were to be made, and learned that by heavy, steady pressure of the breast, thus augmented by heavy weight, they could fracture more evenly than by blow of stone, ax or hammer. They learned that two could work together in stone chipping and do better work than one. Old Mok would hold the forming weapon-head in one hand and the horn-hafted chisel in another, pressing the blade close against the stone and at just such angle as would secure the result he sought, while Ab, advised as to the force of each succeeding stroke, tapped lightly upon the chisel's head. Woe was it for the boy if once he missed his stroke and caught the old man's fingers! Very delicate became the chipping done by these two artists, and excellent beyond any before made were the axes and spearheads produced by what, in modern times, would have been known under the title of "Old Mok & Co."

At this time, too, Ab took lessons in making all the varied articles of elk or reindeer horn and the drinking cups from the horns of urus and aurochs. Old Mok even went so far as to attempt teaching the youth something of carving figures upon tusks and shoulder blades, but in this art Ab never greatly excelled. He was too much a creature of action. The bone needles used by Red-Spot in making skin garments he could form readily enough and he made whistles for Bark and Beech-leaf, but his inclinations were all toward larger things. To become a fighter and a hunter remained his chief ambition.

Rather keen, with light snows but nipping airs, were the winters of this country of the cave men, and there were articles of food essential to variety which were, necessarily,

stored before the cold season came. There
were roots which were edible and which could
be dried, and there were nuts in abundance,
beyond all need. Beechnuts and acorns were
gathered in the autumn, the children at this
time earning fully the right of home and food,
and the stores were heaped in granaries dug
into the cave's sides. Should the snow at any
time fall too deeply for hunting—though such
an occurrence was very rare—or should any
other cause, such, for instance, as the appearance of the great cave tiger in the region,
make the game scarce and hunting perilous,
there was the recourse of nuts and roots and
no danger of starvation. There was no fear
of suffering from thirst. Man early learned to
carry water in a pouch of skin and there were
sometimes made rock cavities, after the manner of the cave kettle, where water could be
stored for an emergency. Besieging wild
beasts could embarrass but could not greatly
alarm the family, for, with store of wood and
food and water, the besieged could wait, and
it was not well for the flesh-seeking quadruped
to approach within a long spear-thrust's length
of the cavern's narrow entrance.

The winter following the establishment of

Ab's real companionship with Old Mok, as it chanced, was not a hard one.   There fell snow enough for tracking, but not so deeply as to incommode the hunter.   There had been a wonderful nut-fall in the autumn and the cave was stored with such quantity of this food that there was no chance of real privation.   The ice was clean upon the river and through the holes hacked with stone axes fish were dragged forth in abundance upon the rude bone and stone hooks, which served their purpose far better than when, in summer time, the line was longer and the fish escaped so often from the barbless implements.   It was a great season in all that made a cave family's life something easy and complacent and vastly promotive of the social amenities and the advancement of art and literature—that is, they were not compelled to make any sudden raid on others to assure the means of subsistence, and there was time for the carving of bones and the telling of strange stories of the past.   The elders declared it one of the finest winters they had ever known.

And so Old Mok and Ab worked well that winter and the youth acquired such wisdom that his casual advice to Oak when the two were out together was something worth listening to because of its confidence and ponderosity. Concerning flint scraper, drill, spearhead, ax or bone or wooden haft, there was, his talk would indicate, practically nothing for the boy to learn. That was his own opinion, though, as he grew older, he learned to modify it greatly. With his adviser he had made good weapons and some improvements; yet all this was nothing. It was destined that an accidental discovery should be his, the effect of which would be to change the cave man's rank among living things. But the youth, just now, was greatly content with himself. He was older and more modest when he made his great discovery.

It was when the fire blazed out at night, when all had fed, when the tired people lay about resting, but not ready yet for sleep, and the story of the day's events was given, that Old Mok's ordinarily still tongue would sometimes loosen and he would tell of what happened when he was a boy, or of the strange tales which had been told him of the time long past, the times when the Shell and Cave people were one, times when there were monstrous things abroad and life was hard to keep.

To all these legends the hearers listened won-
deringly, and upon them afterward Ab and
Oak would sometimes speculate together and
question as to their truth.

CHAPTER XII.

OLD MOK'S TALES.

It was worth while listening to Old Mok when he forgot himself and talked and became earnestly reminiscent in telling of what he had seen or had heard when he was young. One day there had been trouble in the cave, for Bark, left in charge, had neglected the fire and it had "gone out," and upon the return of his parents there had been blows and harsh language, and then much pivotal grinding together of dry sticks before a new flame was gained, and it was only after the odor of cooked flesh filled the place and strong jaws were busy that the anger of One-Ear had abated and the group became a comfortable one. Ab had come in hungry and the value of fire, after what had happened, was brought to his mind forcibly. He laid himself down upon the cave's floor near Old Mok, who was fashioning a shaft of some sort, and, as he lay, poked his toes at Beechleaf, who chuckled and gurgled as she rolled about, never for a moment relinquishing a portion of the slender shin bone of a deer, upon the flesh of which the family had fed. It was a short piece but full of marrow, and the child sucked and mumbled away at it in utmost bliss. Ab thought, somehow, of how poor would have been the eating with the meat uncooked, and looked at his hands, still reddened — for it was he who had twisted the stick which made the fire again. ''Fire is good!'' he said to Mok.

The old man kept his flint scraper going for a moment or two before he answered; then he grunted:

''Yes, it's good if you don't get burned. I've been burned,'' and he thrust out an arm upon which appeared a cicatrice.

Ab was interested. ''Where did you get that?'' he queried.

''Far from here, far beyond the black swamp and the red hills that are farther still. It was when I was strong.''

''Tell me about it,'' said the youth.

''There is a fire country,'' answered Old Mok, ''away beyond the swamp and woods and the place of the big rocks. It is a wonderful place. The fire comes out of the ground in long sheets and it is always the same. The rain and the snow do not stop it. Do I not know? Have I not seen it? Did I not get this scar going too near the flame and stumbling and falling against a hot rock almost within it? There is too much fire sometimes!"

The old man continued: "There are many places of fire. They are to the east and south. Some of the Shell People who have gone far down the river have seen them. But the one where I was burned is not so far away as they; it is up the river to the northwest."

And Ab was interested and questioned Old Mok further about the strange region where flames came from the ground as bushes grow, and where snow or water did not make them disappear. He was destined, at a later day, to be very glad that he had learned the little that was told him. But to-night he was intent only on getting all the tales he could from the veteran while he was in the mood. "Tell about the Shell People," he cried, "and who they are and where they came from. They are different from us."

"Yes, they are different from us," said Old Mok, "but there was a time, I have heard it told, when we were like them. The very old men say that their grandfathers told them

that once there were only Shell People anywhere in this country, the people who lived
along the shores and who never hunted nor
went far away from the little islands, because
they were afraid of the beasts in the forests.
Sometimes they would venture into the wood
to gather nuts and roots, but they lived mostly
on the fish and clams.   But there came a
time when brave men were born among them
who said they would have more of the forest
things, and that they would no longer stay
fearfully upon the little islands.   So they
came into the forest and the Cave Men began.
And I think this story true."

"I think it is true," Old Mok continued,
"because the Shell People, you can see, must
have lived very long where they are now.
Up and down the creek where they live and
along other creeks there lie banks of earth
which are very long and reach far back.
And this is not really earth, but is all made
up of shells and bones and stone spearheads
and the things which lie about a Shell Man's
place.   I know, for I have dug into these long
banks myself and have seen that of which I
tell.   Long, very long, must the Shell People
have lived along the creeks and shores to

have made the banks of bones and shells so high."

And Old Mok was right. They talk of us as the descendants of an Aryan race. Never from Aryan alone came the drifting, changing Western being of to-day. But a part of him was born where bald plains were or where were olive trees and roses. All modern science, and modern thoughtfulness, and all later broadened intelligence are yielding to an admission of the fact that he, though of course commingling with his visitors of the ages, was born and changed where he now exists. The kitchen-midden—the name given by scientists to refuse from his dwelling places—the kitchen-middens of Denmark, as Denmark is to-day, alone, regardless of other fields, suffice to tell a wondrous story. Imagine a kitchen-midden, that is to say the detritus of ordinary living in different ages, accumulated along the side of some ancient water course, having for its dimensions miles in length, extending hundreds of yards back from the margin of this creek, of tens and tens of thousands of years ago, and having a depth of often many feet along this water course. Imagine this vast deposit telling the history of a thousand centuries or more, beginning first with the deposit of clams and mussel shells and of the shells of such other creatures as might inhabit this river seeking its way to the North Sea.   Imagine this deposit increasing year after year and century by century, but changing its character and quality as it rose, and the base is laid for reasoning.

At first these creatures who ranged up and down the ancient Danish creek and devoured the clams and periwinkles must have been, as one might say, but little more than surely anthropoid.   Could such as these have migrated from the Asiatic plateaus?

The kitchen-middens tell the early story with greater accuracy than could any writer who ever lifted pen.   Here the creek-loving, ape-like creatures ranged up and down and quelled their appetites.   They died after they had begotten sons and daughters; and to these sons and daughters came an added intelligence, brought from experience and shifting surroundings.   The kitchen-middens give graphic details.   The bottom layer, as has been said, is but of shells.   Above it, in another layer, counting thousands of years in growth, appear the cracked bones of then existing animals and appear also traces of charred wood, showing that primitive man had learned what fire was. And later come the rudely carved bones of the mammoth and woolly rhinoceros and the Irish elk; then come rude flint instruments, and later the age of smoothed stone, with all its accompanying fossils, bones and indications; and so on upward, with a steady sweep, until close to the surface of this kitchen-midden appear the bronze spear, the axhead and the rude dagger of the being who became the Druid and who is an ancestor whom we recognize. From the kitchen-midden to the pinnacle of all that is great to-day extends a chain not a link of which is weak.

"They tell strange stories, too, the Shell People," Old Mok continued, "for they are greater story-tellers than the Cave Men are, more of them being together in one place, and the old men always tell the tales to the children so that they are never forgotten by any of the people. They say that once huge things came out of the great waters and up the creeks, such as even the big cave tiger dare not face. And the old men say that their grandfathers once saw with their own eyes a monster serpent many times as large as the one you two saw, which came swimming up the creek and seized upon the river horses there and devoured them as easily as the cave bear would a little deer. And the serpent seized upon some of the Cave People who were upon the water and devoured them as well, though such as they were but a mouthful to him. And this tale, too, I believe, for the old Shell Men who told me what their grandfathers had seen were not of the foolish sort."

"But of another sort of story they have told me," Mok continued, "I think little. The old men tell of a time when those who went down the river to the greater river and followed it down to the sea, which seems to have no end, saw what no man can see to-day. But they do not say that their grandfathers saw these things. They only say that their grandfathers told of what had been told them by their grandfathers farther back, of a story which had come down to them, so old that it was older than the great trees were, of monstrous things which swam along the shores and which were not serpents, though they had long necks and serpent heads,

because they had great bodies which were
driven by flippers through the water as the
beaver goes with his broad feet. And at the
same time, the old story goes, were great
birds, far taller than a man, who fed where
now the bustards and the capercailzie are.
And these tales I do not believe, though I
have seen bones washed from the riversides
and hillsides by the rains which must have
come from creatures different from those we
meet now in the forests or the waters. They
are wonderful story-tellers, the old men of the
Shell People."

"And they tell other strange stories," continued the old man. "They say that very long
ago the cold and ice came down, and all the
people and animals fled before it, and that the
summer was cold as now the winter is, and
that the men and beasts fled together to the
south, and were there for a long time, but
came back again as the cold and ice went
back. They say, too, that in still later times,
the fireplaces where the flames came out of
great cracks in the earth were in tens of
places where they are in one now, and that,
even in the ice time, the flames came up, and
that the ice was melted and then ran in rivers

to the sea. And these things I do not believe, for how can men tell of what there was so long ago? They are but the gabblings of the old, who talk so much."

Many other stories the veteran told, but what most affected Ab was his account of the vale of fire. He hoped to see it sometime.

CHAPTER XIII.

AB'S GREAT DISCOVERY.

It may be that never in what was destined to be a life of many changes was Ab happier than in this period of his lusty boyhood and early manhood, when there was so much that was new, when he was full of hope and confidence and of ambition regarding what a mighty hunter and great man he would become in time. As the years passed he was not less indefatigable in his experiments, and the day came when a marvelous success followed one of them, although, like most inventions, it was suggested in the most trivial and accidental manner.

It chanced one afternoon that Ab, a young man of twenty now, had returned early from the wood and was lying lazily upon the sward near the cave's entrance, while, not far away, Bark and the still chubby Beechleaf were rolling about. The boy was teasing the girl at times and then doing something to amuse or awe her. He had found a stiff length of twig and was engaged in idly bending the ends together and then letting them fly apart with a snap, meanwhile advancing toward and threatening with the impact the half-alarmed but wholly delighted Beechleaf. Tired of this, at last, Bark, with no particular intent, drew forth from the pouch in his skin cloak a string of sinew, and drawing the ends of the strong twig somewhat nearly together, attached the cord to each, thus producing accidentally a petty bow of most rotund proportions. He found that the string twanged joyously, and, to the delight of Beechleaf, kept twanging it for such time as his boyish temperament would allow a single occupation. Then he picked from the ground a long, slender pencil of white wood, a sliver, perhaps, from the making of a spear shaft, and began strumming with it upon the taut sinew string. This made a twang of a new sort, and again the boy and girl were interested temporarily. But, at last, even this variation of amusement with the new toy became monotonous, and Bark ceased strumming and began a series of boyish experiments with his plaything. He put one end of the stick against the string and pushed it back until the other end would press against the inside of the twig, and the result would be a taut, new figure in wood and string which would keep its form even when laid upon the ground. Bark made and unmade the thing a time or two, and then came great disaster. He had drawn the little stick, so held in the way we now call arrowwise, back nearly to the point where its head would come inside the bent twig and there fix itself, when the slight thing escaped his hands and flew away.

The quiet of the afternoon was broken by a piercing childish yell which lacked no element of earnestness. Ab leaped to his feet and was by the youngsters in a moment. He saw the terrified Beechleaf standing, screaming still, with a fat arm outheld, from which dangled a little shaft of wood which had pierced the flesh just deeply enough to give it hold. Bark stood looking at her, astonished and alarmed. Understanding nothing of the circumstances, and supposing the girl's hurt came from Bark's careless flinging of sticks toward her, Ab started toward his brother to administer one of those buffets which were so easy to give or get among cave children. But Bark darted behind a convenient tree and there shrieked out his innocence of dire intent, just as the boy of to-day so fluently defends

himself in any strait where castigation looms
in sight.   He told of the queer plaything he
had made, and offered to show how all had
happened.

Ab was doubtful but laughing now, for the
little shaft, which had scarcely pierced the
skin of Beechleaf's arm had fallen to the
ground and that young person's fright had
given way to vengeful indignation and she was
demanding that Bark be hit with something.
He allowed the sinner to give his proof. Bark,
taking his toy, essayed to show how Beechleaf
had been injured.   He was the most unfortu-
nate of youths.   He succeeded but too well.
The mimic arrow flew again and the sound
that rang out now was not the cry of a child.
It was the yell of a great youth, who felt a
sudden and poignant hurt, and who was not
maintaining any dignity.   Had Bark been as
sure of hand and certain of aim as any archer
who lived in later centuries he could not have
sent an arrow more fairly to its mark than he
sent that admirable sliver into the chest of his
big brother. For a second the culprit stood
with staring eyes, then dropped his toy and
flew into the forest with a howl which beto-

kened his fear of something little less than sudden death.

Ab's first impulse was to pursue his sinful younger brother, but, after the first leap, he checked himself and paused to pluck away the thing which, so light the force that had impelled it, had not gone deeply in. He knew now that Bark was really blameless, and, picking up the abandoned plaything, began its examination thoughtfully and curiously.

The young man's instinct toward experiment exhibited itself as usual and he put the splinter against the string and drew it back and let it fly as he had seen Bark do—that promising sprig, by the way, being now engaged in peering from the wood and trying to form an estimate as to whether or not his return was yet advisable. Ab learned that the force of the bent twig would throw the sliver farther than he could toss it with his hand, and he wondered what would follow were something like this plaything, the device of which Bark had so stumbled upon, to be made and tried on a greater scale. "I'll make one like it, only larger," he said to himself.

The venturesome but more or less diplomatic Bark had, by this time, emerged from the wood and was apprehensively edging up toward the place where Ab was standing. The older brother saw him and called to him to come and try the thing again and the youngster knew that he was safe. Then the two toyed with the plaything for an hour or two and Ab became more and more interested in its qualities. He had no definite idea as to its possibilities. He thought only of it as a curious thing which should be larger.

The next day Ab hacked from a low-limbed tree a branch as thick as his finger and about a yard in length, and, first trimming it, bent it as Bark had bent the twig and tied a strong sinew cord across. It was a not discreditable bow, considering the fact that it was the first ever made, though one end was smaller than the other and it was rough of outline. Then Ab cut a straight willow twig, as long nearly as the bow, and began repeating the experiments of the day before. Never was man more astonished than this youth after he had drawn the twig back nearly to its head and let it go!

So drawn by a strong arm, the shaft when released flew faster and farther than the maker of what he thought of chiefly as a thing of sport had imagined could be possible. He had long to search for the headless arrow and when he found it he went away to where were bare open stretches, that he might see always where it fell. Once as he sent it from the string it struck fairly against an oak and, pointless as it was, forced itself deeply into the hard brown bark and hung there quivering. Then came to the youth a flash of thought which had its effect upon the ages: "What if there had been a point to the flying thing and it had struck a reindeer or any of the hunted animals?"

He pulled the shaft from the tree and stood there pondering for a moment or two, then suddenly started running toward the cave. He must see Old Mok!

The old man was at work and alone and the young man told him, somewhat excitedly, why he had thus come running to him. The elder listened with some patience but with a commiserating grin upon his face. He had heard young men tell of great ideas before, of a new and better way of digging pits, or of fishing, or making deadfalls for wild beasts. But he listened and yielded finally to Ab's earnest demand that he should hobble out into the open and see with his own eyes how the strung bow would send the shaft. They went together to an open space, and again and again Ab showed to his old friend what the new thing would do. With the second shot there came a new light into the eyes of the veteran hunter and he bade Ab run to the cave and bring back with him his favorite spear. The young man was back as soon as strong legs could bring him, and when he burst into the open he found Mok standing a long spear's cast from the greatest of the trees which stood about the opening.

"Throw your spear at the tree," said Mok. "Throw strongly as you can."

Ab hurled the spear as the Zulu of later times might hurl his assagai, as strongly and as well, but the distance was overmuch for spear throwing with good effect, and the flint point pierced the wood so lightly that the weight of the long shaft was too great for the holding force and it sank slowly to the ground and pulled away the head. A wild beast struck by the spear at such distance would have been sorely pricked, but not hurt seriously.

"Now take the plaything," said Old Mok,

"and throw the little shaft at the tree with that."

Ab did as he was told, and, poor marksman with his new device, of course missed the big tree repeatedly, broad as the mark was, but when, at last, the bolt struck the hard trunk fairly there was a sound which told of the sharpness of the blow and the headless shaft rebounded back for yards. Old Mok looked upon it all delightedly.

"It may be there is something to your plaything," he said to the young man. "We will make a better one. But your shaft is good for nothing. We will make a straighter and stronger one and upon the end of it will put a little spearhead, and then we can tell how deeply it will go into the wood. We will work."

For days the two labored earnestly together, and when they came again into the open they bore a stronger bow, one tapered at the end opposite the natural tapering of the branch, so that it was far more flexible and symmetrical than the one they had tried before. They had abundance of ash and yew and these remained the good bow wood of all the time of archery. And the shaft was straight and bore a miniature spearhead at its end. The thought of notching the shaft to fit the string came naturally and inevitably. The bow had its first arrow.

An old man is not so easily affected as a young one, nor so hopeful, but when the second test was done the veteran Mok was the wilder and more delighted of the two who shot at the tree in the forest glade. He saw it all! No longer could the spear be counted as the thing with which to do most grievous hurt at a safe distance from whatever might be dangerous. With the better bow and straighter shaft the marksmanship improved; even for these two callow archers it was not difficult to hit at a distance of a double spear's cast the bole of the huge tree, two yards in width at least. And the arrow whistled as if it were a living thing, a hawk seeking its prey, and the flint head was buried so deeply in the wood that both Mok and Ab knew that they had found something better than any weapon the cave men had ever known!

There followed many days more of the eager working of the old man and the young one in the cave, and there was much testing of the new device, and finally, one morning.

Ab issued forth armed with his ax and knife, but without his spear.   He bore, instead, a bow which was the best and strongest the two had yet learned to fashion, and a sheaf of arrows slung behind his back in a quiver made of a hollow section of a mammoth's leg bone which had long been kicked about the cave. The two workers had drilled holes in the bone and passed thongs through and made a wooden bottom to the thing and now it had found its purpose.   The bow was rude, as were the arrows, and the archer was not yet a certain marksman, though he had practiced diligently, but the bow was stiff, at least, and the arrows had keen heads of flint and the arms of the hunter were strong as was the bow.

There was a weary and fruitless search for game, but late in the afternoon the youth came upon a slight, sheer descent, along the foot of which ran a shallow but broad creek, beyond which was a little grass-grown valley, where were feeding a fine herd of the little deer.   They were feeding in the direction of the creek and the wind blew from them to the hunter, so that no rumor of their danger was carried to them on the breeze.   Ab concealed himself among the bushes on the little height

and awaited what might happen.   The herd
fed slowly toward him.

As the deer neared the creek they grouped
themselves together about where were the
greenest and richest feeding-places, and when
they reached the very border of the stream
they were gathered in a bunch of half a hundred, close together.   They were just beyond
a spear's cast from the watcher, but this was
a test, not of the spear, but of the bow, and
the most inexperienced of archers, shooting
from where Ab was hidden, must strike some
one of the beasts in that broad herd.   Ab
sprang to his feet and drew his arrow to the
head.   The deer gathered for a second in
affright, crowding each other before the wild
bursting away together, and then the bowstring twanged, and the arrow sang hungrily,
and there was the swift thud of hundreds of
light feet, and the little glade was almost
silent.   It was not quite silent, for, floundering in its death struggles, was a single deer,
through which had passed an arrow so fiercely
driven that its flint head projected from the
side opposite that which it had entered.

Half wild with triumph was the youth who
bore home the arrow-stricken quarry, and not

much more elated was he than the old man, who heard the story of the hunt, and who recognized, at once far more clearly than the younger one, the quality of the new weapon which had been discovered; the thing destined to become the greatest implement both of chase and warfare for thousands of years to come, and which was to be gradually improved, even by these two, until it became more to them than they could yet understand.

But the lips of each of the two makers of the bow were sealed for the time. Ab and Old Mok cherished together their mighty secret

CHAPTER XIV.

A LESSON IN SWIMMING.

AB and Oak, ranging far in their hunting expeditions, had, long since, formed the acquaintance of the Shell People, and had even partaken of their hospitality, though there was not much to attract a guest in the abodes of the creek-haunters. Their homes were but small caves, not much more than deep burrows, dug here and there in the banks, above high water mark, and protected from wild beasts by the usual heaped rocks, leaving only a narrow passage. This insured warmth and comparative safety, but the homes lacked the spaciousness of the caves and caverns of the hills, and the food of fish and clams and periwinkles, with flesh and fruit but seldom gained, had little attraction for the occasional cave visitor. Ab and Oak would sometimes traffic with the Shell People, exchanging some creature of the land for a product of the water, but they made brief stay in a locality where the food and odors were not quite to their accustomed taste. Yet the settlement had a slight degree of interest to them. They had noted the buxom quality of some of the Shell maidens, and the two had now attained an age when a bright-eyed young person of the other sex was agreeable to look upon. But there had been no love passages. Neither of the youths was yet so badly stricken.

There came an autumn morning when Ab and Oak, who had met at daybreak, determined to visit the Shell People and go with them upon a fishing expedition. The Shell People often fished from boats, and the boats were excellent. Each consisted of four or five short logs of the most buoyant wood, bound firmly together with tough withes, but the contrivance was more than a simple raft, because, at the bow, it had been hewed to a point, and the logs had been so chosen that each curved upward there. It had been learned that the waves sometimes encountered could so more easily be cleft or overridden. None of these boats could sink, and the man of the time was quite at home in the water. It was fun for the young men whose tale is told here to go with the Shell People and assist in spearing fish or drawing them from the river's depths upon rude hooks, and the Shell People did not object, but were rather proud of the attendance of representatives of the hillside aristocracy.

The morning was one to make men far older than these two most confident and full of life. The season was late, though the river's waters were not yet cold. The mast had already begun to fall and the nuts lay thickly among the leaves. Every morning, and more regularly than it comes now, there was a spread of glistening hoar frost upon the lowlands and the little open lands in the forest and upon every spot not tree-protected. At such times there appeared to the eyes of the cave people the splendor of nature such as we now can hardly comprehend. It came most strikingly in spring and autumn, and was something wonderful. The cave men, probably, did not appreciate it. They were accustomed to it, for it was part of the record of every year. Doubtless there came a greater vigor to them in the keen air of the hoar frost time, doubtless the step of each was made more springy and each man's valor more defined in this choice atmosphere. Temperate, with a wonderful keenness to it, was the climate of the cave region in the valley of the present Thames. Even in the days of the cave men, the Gulf Stream, swinging from the equator in the great warm current already formed, laved the then peninsula as it now laves the British Isles. The climate, as has been told, was almost as equable then as now, but with a certain crispness which was a heritage from the glacial epoch. It was a time to live in, and the two were merry on their journey in the glittering morning.

The young men idled on their way and wasted an hour or two in vain attempts to approach a feeding deer nearly enough for effective spear-throwing. They were late when, after swimming the creek, they reached the Shell village and there learned that the party had already gone. They decided that they might, perhaps, overtake the fishermen, and so, with the hunter's easy lope, started briskly down the river bank. They were not destined to fish that day.

Three or four miles had been passed and a straight stretch of the river had been attained, at the end of which, a mile away, could be seen the boats of the Shell People, to be lost to sight a moment later as they swept around a bend. But there was something else in sight. Perched comfortably upon a rock, the sides of which were so precipitous that they afforded a foothold only for human beings, was a young woman of the Shell People who had before attracted Ab's attention and something of his admiration. She was fishing diligently. She had been left by the fishing party, to be taken up on their return, because, in the rush of waters about the base of the rock, was a haunt of a small fish esteemed particularly, and because the girl was one of the little tribe's adepts with hook and line. She raised her eyes as she heard the patter of footsteps upon the shore, but did not exhibit any alarm when she saw the two young men. The ordinary young woman of the Shell People did not worry when away from land. She could swim like an otter and dive like a loon, and of wild beasts she had no fear when she was thus safely bestowed away from the death-harboring forest. The maiden on the rock was most serene.

The young men called to her, but she made no answer. She but fished away demurely, from time to time hauling up a flashing finny thing, which she calmly bumped on the rock and then tossed upon the silvery heap, which had already assumed fair dimensions, close behind her.   As Ab looked upon the young fisherwoman his interest in her grew rapidly and he was silent, though Oak called out taunting words and asked her if she could not talk.   It was not this young woman, but another, who had most pleased Oak among the girls of the Shell People.

It was not love yet with Ab, but the maiden interested him.   He held no defined wish to carry her away to a new home with him, but there arose a feeling that he wanted to know her better.   There might,—he didn't know— be as good wives among the Shell maidens as among the well-running girls of the hills.

"I'll swim to the rock!" he said to his companion, and Oak laughed loudly.

Short time elapsed between decision and action in those days, and hardly had Ab spoken when he flung his fur covering into the hands of Oak, and, clad only in the clout about his hips, dropped, with a splash, into the water.   All this time the girl had been eyeing every motion closely.   As the little waves rose laughingly about the man, she descended lightly from her perch and slid into the stream as easily and silently as a beaver might have done. And then began a chase. The girl, finding mid-current swiftly, was a full hundred yards ahead as Ab came fairly in her wake.

A splendid swimmer was the stalwart young man of the hills. He had been in and out of water almost daily since early childhood, and, though there had never been a test, was confident that, among all the Shell People, there was none he could not overtake, despite what he had heard and knew of their wonderful cleverness in the water. Were not his arms and legs longer and stronger than theirs and his chest deeper? He felt that he could outswim easily any bold fisherman among them, and as for this girl, he would overtake her very quickly and draw her to the bank, and then there would be an interview of much enjoyment, at least to him. His strong arm swept the water back, and his strong legs, working with them, drove his body forward swiftly toward the brown object not very far ahead. Along the bank ran the laughing and shouting Oak.

Yard by yard, Ab's mighty strokes brought him nearer the object of his pursuit. She was swimming breast forward, as was he—for that was his only way—she with a dog-like paddling stroke, and often she turned her head to look backward at the man. She did not, even yet, appear affrighted, and this Ab wondered at, for it was seldom that a girl of the time, thus hunted, was not, and with reason, terrified. She, possibly, understood that the chase did not involve a real abduction, for she and her pursuer had often met, but there was, at least, reason enough for avoiding too close contact on this day. She swam on steadily, and, as steadily, Ab gained upon her.

Down the long stretch of tumbling river, sweeping eastward between hill and slope and plain and woodland, went the chase, while the panting and cheering Oak, strong-legged and enduring as he was, barely kept pace with the two heads he could see bobbing, not far apart now, in the tossing waters. Ab had long since forgotten Oak. He had forgotten how it was that he came to be thus swimming in the river. His thought was only what now made up an overmastering aim. He must reach and seize upon the girl before him!

Closer and closer, though she as much as

he was aided by the swift current, the young man approached the girl. The hundred yards had lessened into tens and he could plainly see now the wake about her and the occasional up-flip of her brown heels as she went high in her stroke. He now felt easily assured of her and laughed to himself as he swept his arms backward in a fiercer stroke and came so close that he could discern her outline through the water. It was but a matter of endurance, he chuckled to himself. How could a woman outswim a man like him?

It was just at the time when this thought came that Ab saw the Shell girl lift her head and turn it toward him and laugh—laugh recklessly, almost in his very face, so close together were they now. And then she taught him something! There was a dip such as the otter makes when he seeks the depths and there was no longer a girl in sight! But this was only a demonstration, made in sheer audacity and blithesome insolence, for the brown head soon appeared again some yards ahead and there was another twist of it and another merry laugh. Then the neat body turned upon its side, and with quick outdriving leg-strokes and the overhand and underhand pull-

ing-forward which modern swimmers partly
know, the girl shot ahead through the tiny
white-capped waves and away from the swimmer so close behind her, as to-day the cutter
leaves the scow.   From the river bank came
a wild yelp, the significance of which, if anal-
ized, might have included astonishment and
great delight and brotherly derision.   Oak was
having a great day of it!   He was the sole
witness of a swimming-match the like of which
was rare, and he was getting even with his
friend for various assumptions of superiority in
various doings.

Unexhausted and sturdy and stubborn, Ab
was not the one to abandon his long chase
because of this new phase of things.   He inhaled a great breath and made the water foam
with his swift strokes, but as well might a wild
goose chase a swallow on the wing as he seek
to overtake that brown streak on the water.
It was wonderful, the manner in which that
Shell girl swam!   She was like the birds which
swim and dive and dip, and know of nothing
which they fear if only they are in the water
far enough away from where there is the need
of stalking over soil and stone.   It was not
that the Shell girl was other than at home on

land. She was quite at home there and reasonably fleet, but the creek and river had so
been her element from babyhood that the
chase of the hill man had been, from the
start, a sheer absurdity.

Ab lifted himself in the waters and gazed
upon the dark spot far away, and, piqued and
maddened, put forth all the swimming strength
there was left in his brawny body. It seemed
for a brief time that he was almost equal to
the task of gaining upon what was little more
than a dot upon the surface far ahead. But
his scant prospect of success was only momentary. The trifling spot in the distant drifts of
the river seemed to have certain ideas of its
own. The speed of its course in the water did
not abate and, in a moment, it was carried
around the bend, and lost to sight. Ab drifted
to the turn and saw, below, a girl clambering
into safety among the rafts of the fishing Shell
People. What she would tell them he did
not know. That was not a matter to be much
considered.

There was but one thing to be done and
that was to reach the land and return to a life
more strictly earthly and more comfortable.
There is nothing like water for overcoming a

young man's fancy for many things. Ab swam now with a somewhat tired and languid stroke to the shore, where Oak awaited him hilariously. They almost came to blows that afternoon, and blows between such as they might have easily meant sudden death. But they were not rivals yet and there was much to talk of good-naturedly, after some slight outflamings of passion on the part of Ab, and the two men were good friends again.

The sum of all the day was that there had been much exercise and fun, for Oak at least. Ab had not caught the Shell girl, manfully as he had striven. Had he caught her and talked with her upon the river bank it might have changed the current of his life. With a man so young and sturdy and so full of life the laughing fancy of a moment might have changed into a stronger feeling and the swimming girl might have become a woman of the cave people, one not quite so equal by heritage to the task of breeding good climbing and running and fighting and progressive beings as some girl of the hills.

It matters little what might have happened had the outcome of the day's effort been the reverse of what it was. This is but the account of the race and what the sequel was when Ab swam so far and furiously and well. It was his first flirtation. It was yet to come to him that he should be really in love in the cave man's way

CHAPTER XV.

THE MAMMOTH AT BAY.

IT was late autumn, and a light snow covered the ground, when one day a cave man, panting for breath, came running down the river bank and paused at the cave of One-Ear. He had news, great news! He told his story hurriedly, and then was taken into the cave and given meat, while Ab, seizing his weapons, fled downward further still toward the great kitchen-midden of the Shell People. Just as ages and ages later, not far from the same region, some Scottish runner carried the fiery cross, Ab ran exultingly with the news it was his to bring. There must be an immediate gathering, not only of the cave men, but of the Shell People as well, and great mutual effort for great gain. The mammoths were near the point of the upland!

The runner to the cave of One-Ear was a hunter living some miles to the north, upon a ledge of a broad forest-covered plateau terminating on the west in a slope which ended in a precipice with more than a hundred feet of sheer descent to the valley below. On rare occasions a herd of mammoths invaded the forest and worked itself toward the apex of the plateau, and then word went all over the region, for it was an event in the history of the cave men. If but a sufficient force could be suddenly assembled, food in abundance for all was almost certainly assured. The prize was something stupendous, but prompt action was required, and there might be tragedies. As bees hum and gather when their hive is disturbed, so did the Shell People when Ab burst in upon them and delivered his message. There was rushing about and a gathering of weapons and a sorting out of men who should go upon the expedition. But little time was wasted. Within half an hour Ab was straining back again up the river toward his own abode, while behind him trailed half a hundred of the Shell People, armed in a way effective enough, but which, in the estimation of the cave men, was preposterous. The spears of the Shell People had shafts of different wood and heads of different material from those of the cave men, and they used their weapons in a different

manner. Accustomed to the spearing of fish
or of an occasional water beast, like a small
hippopotamus, which still existed in the rivers
of the peninsula, they always threw their
spears—though the cave people were experts
with this as well—and, as a last resource in
close conflict, they used no stone ax or mace,
but simply ran away, to throw again from a
distance, or to fly again, as conditions made
advisable. But they were brave in a way—
it was necessary that all who would live must
have a certain animal bravery in those days—
and their numbers made them essential in the
rare hunting of the mammoth.

When the company reached the home of
Ab they found already assembled there a score
of the hill men, and, as the word had gone
out in every direction, it was found, when the
rendezvous was reached, which was the cave
of Hilltop, the man living near the crest of
the plateau, and the one who had made the
first run down the river, that there were more
than a hundred, counting all together, to
advance against the herd and, if possible,
drive the great beasts toward the precipice.
Among this hundred there was none more delighted than Ab and Oak, for, of course, these

two had found each other in the group, and were almost like a brace of dogs whining for the danger and the hunt.

Not lightly was an expedition against a herd of mammoths to be begun, even by a hundred well-armed people of the time of the cave men. The mammoth was a monster beast, with perhaps somewhat less of sagaciousness than the modern elephant, but with a temper which was demoniacal when aroused, and with a strength which nothing could resist. He could be slain only by strategy. Hence the everlasting watch over the triangular plateau and the gathering of the cave and river people to catch him at a disadvantage. But, even with a drove feeding near the slope which led to the precipice, the cave men would have been helpless without the introduction of other elements than their weapons and their clamor. The mammoth paid no more attention to the cave man with a spear than to one of the little wild horses which fed near him at times. The pygmy did not alarm him, but did the pygmy ever venture upon an attack, then it was likely to be seized by the huge trunk and flung against rock or tree, to fall crushed and mangled, or else it was trodden viciously under foot. From one thing, though, the mammoth, huge as he was, would flee in terror. He could not face the element of fire, and this the cave men had learned to their advantage. They could drive the mammoth when they dare not venture to attack him, and herein lay their advantage.

Under direction of the veteran hunter, Hill-top, who had discovered the whereabouts of the drove, preparations were made for the dangerous advance, and the first thing done was the breaking off of dry roots of the over-turned pitch pines, and gathering of knots of the same trees, with limbs attached, to serve as handles. These roots and knots, once lighted, would blaze for hours and made the most perfect of natural torches. Lengths of bark of certain other trees when bound together and lighted at one end burned almost as long and brightly as the roots and knots. Each man carried an unlighted torch of one kind or another, in addition to his weapons, and when this provision was made the band was stretched out in a long line and a silent advance began through the forest. The herd of mammoths was composed of nineteen, led by a monster even of his kind, and men who had been

watching them all night and during the forenoon said that the herd was feeding very near
the edge of the wood, where it ended on the
slope leading to the precipice.   There was ice
upon the slope and there were chances of a
great day's hunting.   To cut off the mammoths, that is, to extend a line across the uprising peninsula where they were feeding,
would require a line of not more than about
five hundred yards in length, and as there
were more than a hundred of the hunters, the
line which could be formed would be most
effective.   Lighted punk, which preserved fire
and gave forth no odor to speak of, was carried by a number of the men, and the advance
began.

It had been an exhilarating scene when the
cave men and Shell People first assembled
and when the work of gathering material for
the torches was in progress.   So far was the
gathering from the present haunt of the game
that caution had been unnecessary, and there
was talk and laughter and all the open enjoyment of an anticipated conquest.   The light
snow, barely covering the ground, flashed in
the sun, and the hunters, practically impervious to the slight cold, were almost prankish

in their demeanor. Ab and Oak especially were buoyant, This was the first hunt upon the rocky peninsula of either of them, and they were delighted with the new surroundings and eager for the fray to come. All about was talk and laughter, which became general with any slight physical disaster which came to one among the hunters in the climbing of some tree for a promising dead branch or finding a treacherous hollow when assailing the roots of some upturned pine. It was a brisk scene and a lively one, that which occurred that crisp morning in late autumn when the wild men gathered to hunt the mammoth. All was brightness and jollity and noise.

Very different, in a moment, was the condition when the hunters entered the forest and, extended in line, began their advance toward the huge objects of their search. The cave man, almost a wild beast himself in some of his ways, had, on occasion, a footfall as light as that of any animal of the time. The twig scarcely crackled and the leaf scarcely rustled beneath his tread, and when the long line entered the wood the silence of death fell there, for the hunters made no sound, and what

slight sound the woodland had before—the
clatter of the woodpeckers and jays—was
hushed by their advance. So through the
forest, which was tolerably close, the dark
line swept quietly forward until there came
from somewhere a sudden signal, and with a
still more cautious advance and contraction of
the line as the peninsula narrowed the quarry
was brought in sight of all.

Close to the edge of the slope, and separated
by a slight open space from the forest proper,
was an evergreen grove, in which the herd of
monster beasts was feeding. A great bull,
with long up-curling tusks, loomed above
them all, and was farthest away in the grove.
The hunters, hidden in the forest, lay voice-
less and motionless until the elders decided
upon a plan of attack, and then the word was
passed along that each man must fire his
torch.

All along the edge of the wood arose the
flashing of little flames. These grew in magnitude until a line of fire ran clear across the
wood, and the mammoths nearest raised their
trunks and showed signs of uneasiness. Then
came a signal, a wild shout, and at once, with
a yell, the long line burst into the open, each

man waving his flaming torch and rushing toward the grove.

There was a chance—a slight one—that the
whole herd might be stampeded, but this had
rarely happened within the memory of the
oldest hunter. The mammoth, though subject
to panic, did not lack intelligence and when
in a group was conscious of its strength. As
that yell ascended, the startled beasts first
rushed deeper into the grove and then, as the
slope beyond was revealed to them, turned
and charged blindly, all save one, the great
tusker, who was feeding at the grove's outer
verge. They came on, great mountains of
flesh, but swerved as they met the advancing
line of fire and weaved aimlessly up and down
for a moment or two. Then a huge bull, stung
by a spear hurled by one of the hunters and
frantic with fear, plunged forward across the
line and the others followed blindly. Three
men were crushed to death in their passage
and all the mammoths were gone save the big
bull, who had started to rejoin his herd but had
not reached it in time. He was now raging
up and down in the grove, bewildered and
trumpeting angrily. Immediately the hunters

gathered closer together and made their line of fire continuous.

The mammoth rushed out clear of the trees and stood looming up, a magnificent creature of unrivaled size and majesty. His huge tusks shone out whitely against the mountain of dark shaggy hair. His small eyes blazed viciously as he raised his trunk and trumpeted out what seemed either a hoarse call to his herd or a roar of agony over his strait. He seemed for a moment as if about to rush upon the dense line of his tormentors, but the flaming faggots dashed almost in his face by the reckless and excited hunters daunted him, and, as a spear lodged in his trunk, he turned with almost a shriek of pain and dashed into the grove again. Close at his heels bounded the hundred men, yelling like demons and forgetting all danger in the madness of the chase. Right through the grove the great beast crashed and then half turned as he came to the open slope beyond. Running beside him was a daring youth trying in vain to pierce him in the belly with his flint-headed spear, and, as the mammoth came for the moment to a half halt, his keen eyes noted the pygmy, his great trunk shot downward and backward,

picked up the man and hurled him yards away
against the base of a great tree, the body as
it struck being crushed out of all semblance
to man and dropping to the earth a shapeless
lump.   But the fire behind and about the
desperate mammoth seemed all one flame
now, countless spears thrown with all the
force of strong arms were piercing his tough
hide, and out upon the slope toward the precipice the great beast plunged.   Upon his very
flanks was the fire and about him all the stinging danger from the half-crazed hunters.   He
lunged forward, slipped upon the smooth glacial floor beneath him, tried to turn again to
meet his thronging foes and face the ring of
flame, and then, wavering, floundering, moving
wonderfully for a creature of his vast size, but
uncertain as to foothold, he was driven to the
very crest of the ledge, and, scrambling vainly,
carrying away an avalanche of ice, snow and
shrubs, went crashing to his death, a hundred
feet below!

CHAPTER XVI.

THE FEAST OF THE MAMMOTH.

To the right and left of the precipice the fall to the plain below was more gradual, and with exultant yells, the cave and Shell men rushed in either direction, those venturing nearest the sheer descent going down like monkeys, clinging as they went to shrubs and vines, while those who ran to where the drop was a degree more passablé fairly tumbled downward to the plain. In an incredibly short space of time absolute silence prevailed in and about the grove where the scene had lately been so fiercely stirring. In the valley below there was wildest clamor.

It was a great occasion for the human beings of the region. There was no question as to the value of the prize the hunters had secured. Never before in any joint hunting expedition, within the memory of the oldest present, had followed more satisfactory result. The spoil was well worth the great effort that had been made; in the estimation of the time, perhaps worth the death of the hunters who had been killed.   The huge beast lay dead, close to the base of the cliff.   One great, yellow-white, curved tusk had been snapped off and showed itself distinct upon the grass some feet away from the mountain of flesh so lately animated. The sight was one worth looking upon in any age, for, in point of grandeur of appearance, the mammoth, while not as huge as some of the monsters of reptilian times, had a looming impressiveness never surpassed by any beast on the earth's surface.   Though prone and dead he was impressive.

But the cave and Shell men were not so much impressed as they were delighted.   They had come into possession of food in abundance and there would be a feast of all the people of the region, and, after that, abundant meat in many a hut and cave for many a day.   The hunters were noisy and excited.   A group pounced upon the broken tusk—for a mammoth tusk, or a piece of one, was a prize in a cave dwelling—and there was prospect of a struggle, but grim voices checked the wrangle of those who had seized upon this portion of the spoil and it was laid aside, to be appor-

tioned later.   The feast was the thing to be
considered now.

Again swift-footed messengers ran along
forest paths and swam streams and thridded
wood and thicket, this time to assemble, not
the hunters alone, but with them all members
of households who could conveniently and
safely come to the gathering of the morrow,
when the feast of the mammoth would be on.
The messengers dispatched, the great carcass
was assailed, and keen flint knives, wielded by
strong and skillful hands, were soon separating
from the body the thick skin, which was
divided as seemed best to the leaders of the
gathering, Hilltop, the old hunter, for his
special services, getting the chief award in the
division.   Then long slices of the meat were
cut away, fires were built, the hunters ate to
repletion and afterward, with a few remaining
awake as guards, slept the sleep of the healthy
and fully fed.   Not in these modern days
would such preliminary consumption of food
be counted wisest preparation for a feast on
the morrow, but the cave and Shell men were
alike independent of affections of the stomach
or the liver, and could, for days in sequence,
gorge themselves most buoyantly.

The morning came crisp and clear, and, with the morning, came from all directions swiftly moving men and women, elated and hungry and expectant. The first families and all other families of the region were gathering for the greatest social function of the time. The men of various households had already exerted themselves and a score or two of fires were burning, while the odor of broiling meat was fragrant all about. Hunter husbands met their broods, and there was banqueting, which increased as, hour after hour, new groups came in. The families of both Ab and Oak were among those early in the valley, Beechleaf and Bark, wide-eyed and curious, coming upon the scene as a sort of advance guard and proudly greeting Ab. All about was heard clucking talk and laughter, an occasional shout, and ever the cracking of stone upon the more fragile thing, as the monster's roasted bones were broken to secure the marrow in them.

There was hilarity and universal enjoyment, though the assemblage, almost by instinct, divided itself into two groups. The cave men and the Shell men, while at this time friendly, were, as has been indicated, unlike in many tastes and customs and to an extent unlike in appearance. The cave man, accustomed to run like the deer along the forest ways, or to avoid sudden danger by swift upward clambering and swinging along among treetops, was leaner and more muscular than the Shell man, and had in his countenance a more daring and confident expression. The Shell man was shorter and, though brawny of build, less active of movement. He had spent more hours of each day of his life in his rude raft-boat, or in walking slowly with poised spear along creek banks, or, with bent back, digging for the great luscious shell-fish which made a portion of his food, than he had spent afoot and on land, with the smell of growing things in his nostrils. The flavor of the water was his, the flavor of the wood the cave man's. So it was that at the feast of the mammoth the allies naturally and good-naturedly became somewhat grouped, each person according to his kind. When hunger was satisfied and the talking-time came on, those with objects and impulses the same could compare notes most interestedly. Constantly the number of the feasters increased, and by mid-day there was a company of magnitude. Much meat was required to feed such a number, but there were tons of meat in a mammoth, enough to defy the immediate assaults of a much greater assemblage than this of exceedingly healthy people. And the smoke from the fires ascended and these rugged ones ate and were happy.

But there came a time in the afternoon when even such feasters as were assembled on this occasion became, in a measure, content, when this one and that one began to look about, and when what might be called the social amenities of the period began. Veterans flocked together, reminiscent of former days when another mammoth had been driven over this same cliff; the young grouped about different firesides, and there was talk of feats of strength and daring and an occasional friendly grapple. Slender, sinewy girls, who had girls' ways then as now, ate together and looked about coquettishly and safely, for none had come without their natural guardians. Rarely in the history of the cave men had there been a gathering more generally and thoroughly festive, one where good eating had made more good fellowship. Possibly—for all things are relative—there has never occurred an affair of more social importance within the centuries since. Human beings, dangerous ones, were merry and trusting together, and the young looked at each other.

Of course Ab and Oak had been eating in company. They had risked themselves dangerously in the battle on the cliff, had escaped injury and were here now, young men of importance, each endowed with an appetite corresponding with the physical exertion of which he was capable and which he never hesitated to make. The amount either of those young men had eaten was sufficient to make a gourmand, though of grossest Roman times, fairly sick with envy, and they were still eating, though, it must be confessed, with modified enthusiasm. Each held in his hand a smoking lump of flesh from some favored portion of the mammoth and each rent away an occasional mouthful with much content. Suddenly Ab ceased mastication and stood silent, gazing intently at a not unpleasing object a few yards distant.

Two girls stood together near a fire about which were grouped perhaps a dozen people. The two were eating, not voraciously, but with an apparent degree of interest in what they were doing, for they had not been among the early arrivals. It was upon these two that Ab's wandering glance had fallen and had been held, and it was not surprising that he had become so interested. Either of the couple was fitted to attract attention, though a pair more utterly unlike it would be difficult to imagine. One was slight and the other the very reverse, but each had striking characteristics.

They stood there, the two, just as two girls so often stand to-day, the hand of one laid half-caressingly upon the hip of the other. The beaming, broad one was chattering volubly and the slender one listening carelessly. The talking of the heavier girl was interrupted evenly by her mumbling at a juicy strip of meat. Her hunger, it was clear, had not yet been satisfied, and it was as clear, too, that her companion had yet an appetite. The slender one was, seemingly, not much interested in the conversation, but the other chattered on. It was plain that she was a most contented being. She was symmetrical only from the point of view of admirers of the heavily built. She had very broad hips and muscular arms and was somewhat squat of structure. It is hesitatingly to be admitted of this young lady that, sturdy and prepossessing, from a practical point of view, as she might be to the average food-winning cave man, she lacked a certain something which would, to the observant, place her at once in good society. She was an exceedingly hairy young woman. She wore the usual covering of skins, but she would have been well-draped, in moderately temperate weather, had the covering been absent. Either for fashion's sake or comfort, not much weight of foreign texture in addition to her own hirsute and, to a certain extent, graceful, natural garb, was needed. She was a female Esau of the time, just a great, good-hearted, strong and honest cave girl, of the subordinate and obedient class which began thousands of years before did history, one who recognized in the girl who stood beside her a stronger and dominating spirit, and who had been received as a trusted friend and willing assistant. It is so to-day, even among the creatures which are said to have no souls, the dogs especially. But the girl had strength and a certain quick, animal intelligence. She was the daughter of a cave man living not far from the home of old Hilltop, and her name

was Moonface. Her countenance was so
broad and beaming that the appellation had
suggested itself in her jolly childhood.

Very different from Moonface was the slender being who, having eaten a strip of meat,
was now seeking diligently with a splinter for
the marrow in the fragment of bone her father
had tossed toward her. Her father was Hilltop, the veteran of the immediate region and
the hero of the day, and she was called Lightfoot, a name she had gained early, for not in
all the country round about was another who
could pass over the surface of the earth with
greater swiftness than could she. And it was
upon Lightfoot that Ab was looking.

The young woman would have been fair to
look upon, or at least fascinating, to the most
world-wearied and listless man of the present
day. She stood there, easily and gracefully,
her arms and part of her breast, above, and
her legs from about the knees, below, showing
clearly from beneath her covering of skins.
Her deep brown hair, knotted back with a
string of the tough inner bark of some tree,
hung upon the middle of her flat, in-setting
back. She was not quite like any of the other
girls about her. Her eyes were larger and

softer and there was more reflection and variety of expression in them.   Her limbs were
quite as long as those of any of her companions and the fingers and toes, though slenderer,
were quite as suggestive of quick and strong
grasping capabilities, but there was, with all
the proof of springiness and litheness, a certain
rounding out.   The strip of hair upon her legs
below the knees was slight and silken, as was
also that upon her arms.   Yet, undoubted
leader in society as her appearance indicated,
quite aside from her father's standing, there
was in her face, with all its loftiness of air, a
certain blithesomeness which was almost at
variance with conditions.   She was a most
lovable young woman—there could be no
question about that—and Ab had, as he
looked upon her for the first time, felt the fact
from head to heel.   He thought of her as like
the leopard tree-cat, most graceful creature of
the wood, so trim was she and full of elastic-
ity, and thought of her, too, as he looked in
her intelligent face, as higher in another way.
He was somewhat awed, but he was courageous.
He had, so far in life, but sought to get what
he wanted whenever it was in sight.   Now he
was nonplussed.

Presently Lightfoot raised her eyes and they
met those of Ab.   The young people looked
at each other steadily for a moment and then
the glance of the girl was turned away.   But,
meanwhile, the man had recovered himself.
He had been eating, absent-mindedly, a well-
cooked portion of a great steak of the mammoth's choicest part.   He now tore it in twain
and watched the girl intently.   She raised her
eyes again and he tossed her a half of the
smoking flesh.   She saw the movement, caught
the food deftly in one hand as it reached her,
and looked at Ab and laughed.   There was
no mock modesty.   She began eating the
choice morsel contentedly; the two were, in a
manner, now made formally acquainted.

The young man did not, on the instant,
pursue his seeming advantage, the result of an
impulsive bravery requiring a greater effort on
his part than the courage he had shown in
conflict with many a beast of the forest.   He
did not talk to the young woman.   But he
thought to himself, while his blood bubbled in
his veins, that he would find her again; that
he would find her in the wood!   She did not
look at him more, for her people were cluster-
ing about her and this was a great occasion.

Ab was recalled to himself by a hoarse excla-
mation. Oak was looking at him fiercely.
There was no other sound, but the young man
stood gazing fixedly at the place where the
girl had just been lost amid the group about
her. And Ab knew instinctively, as men
have learned to know so well in all the years,
from the feeling which comes to them at such
a time, that he had a rival, that Oak also had
seen and loved this slender creature of the
hillside.

There was a division of the mammoth flesh
and hide and tusks. Ab struggled manfully
for a portion of one of the tusks, which he
wanted for Old Mok's carving, and won it at
last, the elders deciding that he and Oak had
fought well enough upon the cliff to entitle
them to a part of the honor of the spoil, and
Oak opposing nothing done by Ab, though his
looks were glowering. Then, as the sun passed
toward the west, all the people separated to
take the dangerous paths toward their homes.
Ab and Oak journeyed away together. Ab
was jubilant, though doubtful, while the face
of Oak was dark. The heart of neither was
light within him.

CHAPTER XVII.

THE COMRADES.

DRIFTING away in various directions toward their homes the Cave and Shell People still kept in groups, by instinct. Social functions terminated before dark and guests going and coming kept together for mutual protection in those days of the cave bear and other beasts. But on the day of the Feast of the Mammoth there was somewhat less than the usual precaution shown. There were vigorous and well-armed hunters at hand by scores, and under such escort women and children might travel after dusk with a degree of safety, unless, indeed, the great cave tiger, Sabre-Tooth, chanced to be abroad, but he was more rarely to be met than others of the wild beasts of the time. When he came it was as a thunderbolt and there were death and mourning in his trail. The march through the forest as the shadows deepened was most watchful. There was a keen lookout on the part of the men, and the women kept their children well in hand. From time to time, one family after another detached itself from the main body and melted into the forest on the path to its own cave near at hand. Thus Hilltop and his family left the group in which were Ab and Oak, and glances of fire followed them as they went. The two girls, Lightfoot and Moon-face, had walked together, chattering like crows. They had strung red berries upon grasses and had hung them in their hair and around their necks, and were fine creatures. Lightfoot, as was her wont, laughed freakishly at whatever pleased her, and in her merry mood had an able second in her sturdy companion. There were moments, though, when even the irrepressible Lightfoot was thoughtful and so quiet that the girl who was with her wondered. The greater girl had been lightly touched with that unnamable force which has changed men and women throughout all the ages. The picture of Ab's earnest face was in her mind and would not depart. She could not, of course, define her own mood, nor did she attempt it. She felt within herself a certain quaking, as of fear, at the thought of him, and yet, so she told herself again and again, she was not afraid. All the time she could see Ab's face, with its look of longing and possession, but with something else in it, when his eyes met hers, which she could not name nor understand. She could not speak of him, but Moonface had upon her no such stilling influence.

"They look alike," she said.

Lightfoot assented, knowing the girl meant Ab and Oak. "But Ab is taller and stronger," Moonface continued, and Lightfoot assented as indifferently, for, somehow, of the two she had remembered definitely one only. She became daring in her reflections: "What if he should want to carry me to his cave?" and then she tried to run away from the thought and from anything and everybody else, leaping forward, outracing and leaving all the company. She reached her father's cave far ahead of the others and stood, laughing, at the entrance, as the family and Moonface, a guest for the night, came trotting up.

And Ab, the buoyant and strong, was not himself as he journeyed with the homeward-pressing company. His mood changed and he dropped away from Oak and lagged in the rear of the little band as it wound its way through the forest. Slight time was needed for others to recognize his mood, and he was strong of arm and quick of temper, as all knew well, and, so, he was soon left to stalk behind in independent sulkiness. He felt a weight in his breast; a fiery spot burned there. He was fierce with Oak because Oak had looked at Lightfoot with a warm light in his eyes. He! when he should have known that Ab was looking at her! This made rage in his heart; and sadness came, too, because he was perplexed over the girl. "How can I get her?" he mumbled to himself, as he stalked along.

Meanwhile, at the van of the company there was noise and frolic. Assembled in force, they were for the hour free from dread of the haunting terror of wild beasts, and, satisfied with eating, the Cave and Shell People were in one of the merriest moods of their lives, collectively speaking. The young men were especially jubilant and exuberant of demeanor. Their sport was rough and dangerous. There were scuffling and wrestling and the more reckless threw their stone axes, sometimes at each other, always, it is true, with warning cries, but with such wild, unconscious strength put in the throwing that the finding of a living target might mean death. Ab, engrossed in

thoughts of something far apart from the rude
sport about him, became nervously impatient.
Like the girl, he wanted to escape from his
thoughts, and bounding ahead to mingle with
the darting and swinging group in front, he
was soon the swift and stalwart leader in their
foolishly risky sport, the center of the whole
commotion.   One muscled man would hurl
his stone hatchet or strong flint-headed spear
at a green tree and another would imitate him
until a space in advance was covered and the
word given for a rush, when all would race for
the target, each striving to reach it first and
detach his own weapon before others came.
It was a merry but too careless contest, with
a chance of some serious happening.   There
followed a series of these mad games and the
oldsters smiled as they heard the sound of
vigorous contest and themselves raced as they
could, to keep in close company with the
stronger force.

Ab had shown his speed in all his playing.
Now he ran to the front and plucked out his
spear, a winner, then doubled and ran back
beside the pathway to mingle with the central
body of travelers, having in mind only to keep
in the heart and forefront of as many contests

as possible. There was more shouting and
another rush from the main body and, bounding aside from all, he ran to get the chance
of again hurling his spear as well. A great
oak stood in the middle of the pathway and
toward it already a spear or two had been
sent, all aimed, as the first thrower had indicated, at a white fungus growth which protruded from the tree. It was a matter of
accuracy this time. Ab leaped ahead some
yards in advance of all and hurled his spear.
He saw the white chips fly from the side of
the fungus target, saw the quivering of the
spear shaft with the head deep sunken in the
wood, and then felt a sudden shock and pain
in one of his legs. He fell sideways off the
path and beneath the brushwood, as the wild
band, young and old, swept by. He was
crippled and could not walk. He called aloud,
but none heard him amid the shouting of
that careless race. He tried to struggle to his
feet, but one leg failed him and he fell back,
lying prone, just aside from the forest path,
nearly weaponless and the easy prey of the
wild beasts. What had hurt him so grievously
was a spear thrown wildly from behind him.
It had, hurled with great strength, struck a

smooth tree trunk and glanced aside, the point of the spear striking the young man fairly in the calf of the leg, entering somewhat the bone itself, and shocking, for the moment, every nerve. The flint sides had cut a vein or two and these were bleeding, but that was nothing. The real danger lay in his helplessness. Ab was alone, and would afford good eating for those of the forest who, before long, would be seeking him. The scent of the wild beast was a wonderful thing. The man tried to rise, then lay back sullenly. Far in the distance, and growing fainter and fainter, he could hear the shouts of the laughing spearthrowers.

The strong young man, thus left alone to death almost inevitable, did not altogether despair. He had still with him his good stone ax and his long and keen stone knife. He would, at least, hurt something sorely before he was eaten, he thought grimly to himself. And then he pressed leaves together on the cut upon his leg, and laid himself back upon the leaves and waited.

He did not have to wait long. He had not thought to do so. How full the woods were of blood-scenting and man-eating things none knew better than he. His ear, keen and trained, caught the patter of a distant approach. "Wolves," he said to himself at first, and then "Hyenas," for the step was puzzling. He was perplexed. The step was regular, and it was not in the forest on either side, but was coming up the path. A terror came upon him and he had crawled deeper into the shades, when he noted that the steps first ceased, and then that they wandered searchingly and uncertainly. Then, loud and strong, rang out a voice, calling his name, and it was the voice of Oak! He could not answer for a moment, and then he cried out gladly.

Oak had, in the forward-rushing group, seen Ab's hurt and fall, but had thought it a trifling matter, since no outcry came from those behind, and so had kept his course away and ahead with the rest. But finally he had noted the absence of Ab and had questioned, and then—first telling some of his immediate companions that they were to lag and wait for him—had started back upon a run to reach the place where he had last seen his friend. It was easy now to arrange wet leaves about Ab's crippling, but little more than temporary, wound. The two, one leaning upon the other and hobbling painfully, and each with weapons in hand, contrived, at last, to reach Oak's lingering and grumbling contingent. Ab was helped along by two instead of one then, and the rest was easy. When the pathway leading to home was reached, Oak accompanied his friend, and the two passed the night together.

Ab, once on his own bed, with Oak couched beside him, was surprised to find, not merely that his physical pain was going, but that the greater one was gone. The weight and burning had left his breast and he was no longer angry at Oak. He thought blindly but directly toward conclusions. He had almost wanted to kill Oak, all because each saw the charm of and wanted the possession of a slender, beautiful creature of their kind. Then something dangerous had happened to him, and this same Oak, his friend, the man he had wished to kill, had come back and saved his life. The sense which we call gratitude, and which is not unmingled with what we call honor, came to this young cave man then. He thought of many things, worried and wakeful as he was, and perhaps made more acute of perception by the slight, exciting fever of his wound.

He thought of how the two, he and Oak, had planned and risked together, of their boyish follies and failures and successes, and of how, in later years, Oak had often helped him, of how he had saved Oak's life once in the river swamp, where quicksands were, of how Oak had now offset even that debt by carrying him away from certain ending amid wild beasts. No one—and of the cave men he knew many— no one in all the careless, merry party had missed him save Oak. He doubtless could not have told himself why it was, but he was glad that he could repay it all and have the balance still upon his side. He was glad that he had the secret of the bow and arrow to reveal. That should be Oak's! So it came that, late that night, when the fire in the cave had burned low and when one could not wisely speak above a whisper, Ab told Oak the story of the new weapon, of how it had been discovered, of how it was to be used and of all it was for hunters and fighters. Furthermore, he brought his best bow and best arrows forth, and told Oak they were his and that they would practice together in the morning. His astonished and delighted companion had little to say over the revelation. He was eager for the morning, but he straightened out his limbs upon the leafy mattress and slept well. So, somewhat later, did the half-feverish Ab.

Morning came and the cave people were astir. There was brief though hearty feeding and then Ab and Oak and Old Mok, to whom Ab had said much aside, went away from the cave and into the forest. There Oak was taught the potency of the new weapon, its deadly quality and the safety of distance it afforded its user. It was a great morning for all three, not excepting the stern and critical old teacher, when they thus met together in the wood and the secret of what two had found was so transmitted to another. As for Oak, he was fairly aflame with excitement. He was far from slow of mind and he recognized in a moment the enormous advantage of the new way of killing either the things they ate, or the things they dreaded most. He could scarcely restrain his eagerness to experiment for himself. Before noon had come he was gone, carrying away the bow and the good arrows. As he disappeared in the wood Ab said nothing, but to himself he thought:

"He may have all the bows and arrows he can make, but I will have Lightfoot myself!"

Ab and Mok started for the cave again, Ab, bow in hand and with ready arrow. There was a patter of feet upon leaves in the wood beside them and then the arrow was fitted to the string, while Old Mok, strong-armed if weak-legged, raised aloft his spear. The two were seeking no conflict with wild beasts to-day and were but defensive and alert. They were puzzled by the sound their quick ears caught. "Patter, patter," ever beside them, but deep in the forest shade, came the sound of menacing followers of some sort.

There was tension of nerves. Old Mok. sturdy and unconsciously fatalistic, was more self-contained than the youth at his side, bow-armed and with flint ax and knife ready for instant use. At last an open space was reached across which ran the well-worn path. Now the danger must reveal itself. The two men emerged into the glade, and, a moment later, there bounded into it gamboling and full of welcome, the wolf cubs, which had played about the cave so long, who were now detached from their own kind and preferred the companionship of man. There was laughter then, and a more careless demeanor with the weapon borne.

CHAPTER XVIII.

LOVE AND DEATH.

DIFFERENT from his former self became this young forester, Ab. He was thinking of something other than wild beasts and their pursuit. Instinctively, the course of his hunting expeditions tended toward the northwest and soon the impulse changed to a design. He must look upon Lightfoot again! Henceforth he haunted the hill region, and never keener for quarry or more alert for the approach of some dangerous animal was the eye of this woodsman than it was for the appearance somewhere of a slender figure of a cave girl. Neither game nor things to dread were numerous in the vicinity of the home of Hilltop, for there one of the hardiest and wisest among hunters had occupied his cave for many years, and wild beasts learn things. So it chanced that Lightfoot could wander farther afield than could most girls of the time. Ab knew all this well, for the quality of expert and venturesome old Hilltop was familiar to all the cave men throughout a wide stretch of country. So Ab, somewhat shamefaced to his own consciousness, hunted in a region not the best for spoil, and looked for a girl who might appear on some forest path, moderately safe from the rush of any of the hungry man-eaters of the wood.

But not all the time of this wild lover was wasted in haunting the possible idling-places of the girl he wanted so. With love there had come to him such sense and thoughtfulness as has come with earnest love to millions since. What could he do with Lightfoot should he gain her? He was but a big, young fighting man and hunter, still sleeping, almost nightly, on one of the leaf beds in his father's cave. With a wife of his own he must have a cave of his own. Compared with his first impulses toward the girl, this was a new train of thought, and, as we recognize it to-day, a nobler one. He wanted to care for his own. He wanted a cave fit for the reception of such a woman as this, to him, the sweetest and proudest of all beings, Lightfoot, daughter of old Hilltop, of the wooded highlands.

Far up the river, far beyond the home of Oak's father and beyond the shining marsh-

lands and the purple heather reaches which
made the foothills pleasant, extended to the
river's bank a promontory, bold and picturesque
and clad heavily with the best of trees.   It
was a great stretch of land, where, in some of
nature's grim work, the earth had been up-
heaved and there had been raised good soil for
giant forests, and at the same time been made
broad caverns to become future habitations of
the creature known as man.   But the trees
bore nuts and fruits, and such creatures as
found food in nuts and fruits, and, later, such
as loved rich herbage, came to the forest in
great numbers, and then followed such as fed
upon these again, all the flesh eaters, to whom
man was, as any other living thing, to be seized
upon and devoured.   The promontory, so rich
in game and nuts and fruits, was, at the same
time, the most dangerous in all the region for
human habitation.   There were deep, dry
caves within its limits, but in none of them had
a cave man yet ventured to make his home.   It
was toward this promontory that the young
man in love turned his eyes.   Because others
had feared to make a home in this lone, high
region should he also fear?   There was food
there in plenty and if there were chance of

fighting in plenty, so much the better! Was
he not strong and fleet; had he not the best of
spears and axes? Above all, had he not the
new weapon which made man far above the
beasts? Here was the place for a home which
should be the best in all this region of the cave
men. Here game and food of all kinds would be
most abundant. The situation would demand
a brave man and a woman scarcely less courageous, but would not he and the girl he was
determined to bring there meet all occasion?
His mind was fixed.

Ab found a cave, one clean and dry and
opening out upon a slight treeless area, and
this he, lover-like, improved for the woman
he had resolved to bring there, arranging carefully the interior of which must be a home.
He had fancies such as lovers have exhibited
from since the time when the plesiosaurus
swashed away in the strand of a warm sea a
hollow nursery for the birth and first tending
of the young of his odd kind, up to the later
time when men have squandered fortunes on
the sleeping rooms of women they have loved.
He toiled for many days. With his ax he
chipped away the cavern's sharp protuberances
at each side, and with the stone chips from

the walls and with what he brought from outside, he made the floor white and clean and nearly level.   He built a fireplace and chipped into a huge stone, which, fortunately, lay inside the cave, a hollow for holding drinking water, or for the boiling of meat.   He built up a passage-way at the entrance, allowing something but not too much more than his own width, as the gauge for measurement of its breadth.   He brought into the cave a deep carpet of leaves and made a wide bed in one corner and this he covered with furred skins, for many skins Ab owned in his own right. Then, with a thick fragment of tough branch as a lever, he rolled a big stone near the cave's entrance and left it ready to be occupied as a home.   The woman was still lacking.

There came a day when Ab, impatient after his searching and waiting, but yet resolute, had killed a capercailzie—the great grouse-like bird of the time, the descendants of which live to-day in northern forests—and had built a fire and feasted, and then, instinctively careful, had climbed to the first broad, low branch of an enormous tree and there adjusted himself to sleep the sleep of one who has eaten heartily.   He lay with the big branch for a bed, supported on either side by green, upspringing twigs, and slept well for an hour or two and then awoke, lazy and listless, but with much good to him from the repast and rest. It was not yet very late in the afternoon and the sun still shone kindly upon him, as upon a whole world of rejoicing things. Something like a reflection of the life of the morning was beginning to manifest itself, as is ever the way where forests and wild things are. The wonderful noise of wood life was renewed. As the young man awakened, he felt in every pulse the thrilling powers of existence. Everything was fair to look upon. His ears took in the sound of the voices of birds, already beginning vesper songs, though the afternoon was yet so early as scarcely to hint of evening, and the scent from a thousand plants and flowers, permeating and intoxicating, reached his senses as he lounged sprawlingly upon his safe bed aloft.

It was attractive, the scene which Ab looked upon. The forest was in all the glory of summer and nesting and breeding things were happy. There was the fullness of the being of trees and plants and of all birds and beasts. There was a soft commingling of sounds which told of the life about, the effect of which was, somehow, almost drowsy in the blending of all together. The great ferns waved gently along the hollows as the slight breeze touched them. They were queer, those ferns. They were not quite so slender and tapering and gothic as the ferns we see to-day. They were a trifle more lush and ragged, and their tips were sometimes almost rounded. But Ab noted little of fern or bird. It was only the general sensuousness that was upon him. The smell of the pines was a partial tonic to the healthy, half-awakened man, and, though he lay back upon the rugged wooden bed and half dozed again, nature had aroused him a trifle beyond the point of relapse into abso-lute, unknowing slumber. There was coming to him a sharpness of perception which af-fected the quiescence of his enjoyment. He rose to a sitting posture and looked about him. At once his eyes flashed, every nerve and muscle became tense and the blood leaped turbulently in his veins. He had seen that for which he had come into this region, the girl who had so reached his rude, careless heart. Lightfoot was very near him!

The girl, all unconscious, was sitting upon

the trunk of a fallen tree which lay close beside a creek. There was an abundance of
small pebbles upon the little strand and the
young lady was absent-mindedly engaged in an
occupation in which, to the observer, she took
some interest, while she, no doubt, was really
thinking of something else. She sat there,
slender, beautiful and excelling, in her way,
the belle of the period, merely amusing herself. Her toes were charming toes. There
could be no debate on that point, for, while
long and strong and flexible, they had a certain evenness and symmetry. They were
being idly employed just now. At the creek's
edge, half imbedded in the ground, uprose the
crest of a granite stone. Picking up pebble
after pebble in her admirable toes, Lightfoot
was engaged in throwing them, one after another, at the outstanding point of granite,
utilizing in the performance only those toes
and the brown leg below the knee. She did
exceedingly well and hit the red-brown target
often. Ab, hot-headed and fierce lover in the
tree top, looked on admiringly. How perfect
of form was she; how bright the face! and
then, forgetting himself, he cried aloud and
slid from the branch as easily and swiftly as

any serpent and started running toward the girl.   He must have her!

With his cry, the girl leaped to her feet, and as he reached the ground, recognized him on the instant.   She knew in the same instant that they had felt together and that it was not by accident that he was near her. She had felt as he; so far as a woman may feel with a man; but maidens are maidens, and sweet lightness dreads force, and a modified terror came upon her.   She paused for a moment, then turned and ran toward the upland forest.

Not a moment hesitating or faltering as affected by the girl's action was the young man who had tumbled from the tree bed. The blood dancing within him and the great natural impulse of gaining what was greatest to him in life controlled him now.   He was hot with fierce lovingness.   He ran well, but he did not run better than the graceful thing before him.

Even for the critical being of the great cities of to-day, the one who "manages" races of all sorts, it would have been worth while to see this race in the forest.   As the doe leaps, scarcely touching the ground, ran

Lightfoot. As the wolf or hound runs, less swift for the moment, but tireless, ran the man behind her. Yet of all the men in the cave region, this flying girl wanted most this man to take her! It was the maidenly force-dreading instinct alone which made her run.

Ab, dogged and enduring, lost no space as the race led away toward the hill and home of the fleet thing ahead of him. There were miles to be covered, and therein he had hope. They were on the straight path to Hilltop's cave, though there were divergent, curving side paths almost as available; but to avoid her pursuer, the fugitive could take none of these. There were cross-cuts everywhere. In leaving the direct path she would but lose ground. To reach soon enough by straight, clean running the towering wooded hill in which was her father's cave seemed the only hope of the half-unwilling fugitive.

There were descents and ascents in the long chase and plateaus where the running was on level ground. Straining forward, gaining little, but confident of overtaking the girl, Ab, deep-chested and physically untroubled, pressed onward, when he noted that the girl made a sudden spurt and bounded forward

with a speed not shown before, while, at the
same time, she swerved from the right of the
path.

It was not Ab who had made her swerve.
Some new alarm had come to her.   She was
about to reach and, as Ab supposed, pass one
of the inletting paths entering almost at right
angles from the left.   She did not pass it.
She leaped into it in evident terror and then,
breaking out from the wood on the right, came
another form and one surely in swift following.
Ab knew the figure well.   Oak was the new
pursuer!

The awful rage which rose in the heart of
Ab as he saw what was happening is what
can no more be described than one can tell
what a tiger in the jungle thinks.   He saw
another—the other his friend—pursuing and
intending to take what he wanted to be his
and what had become to him more than all
else in the world; more than much eating and
the skins of things to keep him warm, more
than a mammoth's tooth to carve, more than
the glorious skin of the great cave tiger, the
possession of which made a rude nobility, more
than anything and all else!   He leaped aside
from the path.   He knew well the other path

upon which were running Oak and Lightfoot. He knew that he could intercept them, because, though the running was not so good, the distance to be covered was much less, for to him path running was a light matter. In the wood he ran as easily and leaped as well and attained a point almost as quickly as the beasts. There was a stress of effort and, as the shadows deepened, he burst in upon the cross path where he knew were the fleeing Lightfoot and following Oak. He had thought to head them off, but Ab was not the only man who was swift of foot in the cave country. They passed, almost as he bounded from the forest. He saw them close together not many yards ahead of him and, with a shout of rage, bent himself in swift and terrible pursuit again.

It was all plain to Ab now as he flew along, unnoted by the two ahead of him. He knew that Oak had, like him, determined to own Lightfoot, and had like him, been seeking her. Only chance had made the chase thus cross Oak's path; but that made no difference. There must be a grim meeting soon. Ab could see that the endurance of the wonderfully fleet-footed woman was not equal to that of the man so near her. She would soon be overtaken. Before her rose the hill, not a mile in its slope, where were her father's cave, and safety. He knew that she had not the strength to breast it fleetly enough for covert. And, as he looked, he saw the girl turn a frightened face toward her close pursuer and knew that she saw him as well. Her pace slackened for a moment as this revelation came to her, and he felt, somehow, that in him she recognized comparative protection. Then she recovered herself and bent all the power she had toward the ascent. But Oak had been gaining steadily, and now, with a sudden rush, he reached her and grasped her, the woman shrieking wildly. A moment later Ab rushed in upon them with a shout. Instinctively Oak released the girl, for in the cry he heard that which meant menace and immediate danger. As Lightfoot felt herself free she stood for a moment or two without a movement, with wide-open eyes, looking upon what was happening before her. Then she bounded away, not looking backward as she ran.

The two men stood there glaring at each other, Oak perched, and yet not perched, so broad and perfect was his foothold, on the crest of a slight shelf of the downward slope. There stood the two men, poised, the one above, the other below, two who had been as close together from childhood as all the attributes of mind and body might allow, and yet now as far apart as human beings may be. They were beautiful in a way, each in his murderous, unconscious posing for the leap. The sun hit the blue ax of Oak and made it look a gray. The raised ax of Ab, which was of a lighter colored stone, was in the shade and its yellowness was darkened into brown. The ,spectacle lasted for but a second. As Oak leaped Ab bounded aside and they stood upon a level, a tiny plateau, and there was fierce, strong fencing. One could not note its methods; even the keen-eyed wolverine, crouching low upon an adjacent monster limb, could never have followed the swift movements of these stone axes. The dreadful play was brief. The clash of stone together ceased as there came a duller sound, which told that stone had bitten bone. Oak, slightly the higher of the two, as they stood thus in the fray, leaned forward suddenly, his arms aloft, while from his hand dropped the blue ax. He floundered down uncouthly and

grasped the beech leaves with his hands, and
then lay still.   Ab stood there weaponless, a
creature wandering of mind.   His yellow ax
had parted from his hand, sunk deeply into
the skull of Oak, and he looked upon it curiously and vacantly.   He was not sane.   He
stepped forward and pulled the ax away and
lifted it to a level with his eyes and went to
where the sunlight shone.   The ax was not
yellow any more.   Meanwhile a girl was flitting toward her home and the shadows of the
waning day were deepening.

CHAPTER XIX.

A RACE WITH DREAD.

AB looked toward the forest wherein Lightfoot had fled and then looked upon that which
lay at his feet. It was Oak—there were the
form and features of his friend—but, somehow, it was not Oak. There was too much
silence and the blood upon the leaves seemed
far too bright. His rage departed, and he
wanted Oak to answer and called to him, but
Oak did not answer. Then came slowly to
him the idea that Oak was dead and that the
wild beasts would that night devour the dead
man where he lay. The thought nerved him
to desperate, sudden action. He leaped forward, he put his arms about the body and
carried it away to a hollow in the wooded
slope. He worked madly, doing some things
as he had seen the cave people do at other
buryings. He placed the weapons of Oak
beside him. He took from his belt his own
knife, because it was better than that of Oak,
and laid it close to the dead man's hand, and

then, first covering the body with beech leaves, he worked frantically upon the overhanging soil, prying it down with a sharppointed fragment of limb, and tossing in upon all as heavy stones as he could lift, until a great cairn rose above the hunter who would hunt no more.

Panting with his efforts, Ab sat himself down upon a rock and looked upon the monument he had raised. Again he called to Oak, but there was still no answer. The sun had set, evening shadows thickened around him. Then there came upon the live man a feeling as dreadful as it was new, and, with a yell, which was almost a shriek, he leaped to his feet and bounded away in fearful flight.

He only knew this, that there was something hurt his inside of body and soul, but not the inside of him as it had been when once he had eaten poisonous berries or when he had eaten too much of the little deer. It was something different. It was an awful oppression, which seemed to leave his body, in a manner, unfeeling but which had a great dread about it and which made him think and think of the dead man, and made him want to run away and keep running. He had al-

ready run far that day, but he was not tired
now. His legs seemed to have the hard
sinews of the stag in them but up toward the
top of him was something for them to carry
away as fast and far as possible from somewhere. He raced from the dense woodland
down into the broad morass to the west—beyond which was the rock country—and into
which he had rarely ventured, so treacherous
its ways. What cared he now! He made
great leaps and his muscles and sinews responded to the thought of him. To cross
that morass safely required a touch on tus-
socks and an upbounding aside, a zig-zag exhibition of great strength and knowingness
and recklessness. But it was unreasoning; it
was the instinct begotten of long training and,
now, of the absence of all nervousness. Each
taut toe touched each point of bearing just as
was required above the quagmire, and, all un-
perceiving and uncaring, he fled over dirty
death as easily as he might have run upon
some hardened woodland pathway. He did
not think nor know nor care about what he
was doing. He was only running away from
the something he had never known before!
Why should he be running now? He had

killed things before and not cared and had forgotten. Why should he care now? But there was the something which made him run. And where was Oak? Would Oak meet him again and would they hunt together? No, Oak would not come, and he, this Ab, had made it so! He must run. No one was following him—he knew that—but he must run!

The marsh was passed, night had fallen, but he ran on, pressing into the bear and tiger haunted forest beyond. Anything, anything, to make him forget the strange feeling and the thing which made him run! He plunged into a forest path, utterly reckless, wanting relief, a seeker for whatever might come.

In that age and under such conditions as to locality it was inevitable that the creature, man, running through such a forest path at night, must face some fierce creature of the carnivora seeking his body for food. Ab, blinded of mood, cared not for and avoided not a fight, though it might be with the monster bear or even the great tiger. There was no reason in his madness. He was, though he knew it not, a practical suicide, yet one who would die fighting. What to him were weight and strength to-night? What to him were such encounters as might come with hungry four-footed things? It would but relieve him were some of the beasts to try to gain his life and eat his body. His being seemed valueless, and as for the wild beasts— and here came out the splendid death-facing quality of the cave man—well, it would be odd if there were not more deaths than one! But all this was vague and only a minor part of thought.

Sometimes, as if to invite death, he yelled as he ran. He yelled whenever in his fleeting visions he saw Oak lying dead again. So ran the man who had killed another.

There was a growl ahead of him, a sudden breaking away of the bushes, and then he was thrown back, stunned and bleeding, because a great paw had smitten him. Whatever the beast might be, it was hungry and had found what seemed easy prey. There was a difference, though, which the animal,—it was doubtless a bear—unfortunately for him, did not comprehend, between the quality of the being he proposed to eat just now and of other animals included in his ordinary menu. But the bear did not reason; he but plunged forward to crush out the remaining life of the runner his great paw had driven back and down and then to enjoy his meal.

The man was little hurt. His skin coat had somewhat protected him and his sinewy body had such toughness that the hurling of it backward for a few feet was not anything involving a fatality. Very surely and suddenly had been thrust upon him now the practical lesson of being or dying, and it was good for the half-crazed runner, for it cleared his mind. But it made him no less desperate or careless. With strength almost maniacal he leaped at what he would have fled from at any other time, and, swinging his ax with the quickness of light, struck tremendously at the great lowering head. He yelled again as he felt stone cut and crash into bone, though himself swept aside once more as a great paw, side-struck, hurled him into the bushes. He bounded to his feet and saw something huge and dark and gasping floundering in the pathway. He thought not but ran on panting. By some strange freak of forest fortune abetting might the man wandering of mind had driven his ax nearly to the haft into the skull of his huge assailant. It may be that never

before had a cave man, thus armed, done so
well. The slayer ran on wildly, and now
weaponless.

Soon to the runner the scene changed. The
trees crowded each other less closely and
there was less of defined pathway. There
came something of an ascent and he breasted
it, though less swiftly, for, despite the impel-
ling force, nature had claims, and muscles were
wearying of their work. Fewer and fewer
grew the trees. He knew that he was where
there was now a sweep of rocky highlands and
that he was not far from the Fire Country, of
which Old Mok had so often told him. He
burst into the open, and as he came out under
the stars, which he could see again, he heard
an ominous whine, too near, and a distant
howl behind him. A wolf pack wanted him.

He shuddered as he ran. The life instinct
was fully awakened in him now, as the dread
from which he had run became more distant.
Had he heard that close whine and distant
howl before he fairly reached the open he
would have sought a treetop for refuge. Now
it was too late. He must run ahead blindly
across the treeless space for such harborage
as might come. Far ahead of him he could

see light, the light of fire, reaching out toward him through the darkness. He was panting and wearied, but the sounds behind him were spur enough to bring the nearly dead to life. He bowed his head and ran with such effort as he had never made before in all his wild and daring existence.

The wolves of the time, greater, swifter and fiercer than the gaunt gray wolves of northern latitudes and historic times, ran well, but so did contemporaneous man run well, and the chase was hard. With his life to save, Ab swept panting over the rocky ground with a swiftness begotten of the grand last effort of remaining strength, running straight toward the light, while the wolf pack, now gathered, hurled itself from the wood behind and followed swiftly and relentlessly. Ever before the man shone the light more brightly; ever behind him became more distinct the sound made by the following pack. It was a dire strait for the running man. He was no longer thinking of what he had lately done. He ran.

The light he had seen extended as he neared it into what looked like a great fence of flame lying across his way. There were gaps in the fence where the flame, still continuous, was not so high as elsewhere. He did not hesitate. He ran straight ahead. Closer and closer behind him crowded the pursuing wolves, and straight at the flame he ran. There was one chance in many, he thought, and he took it without hesitation. Close before him now loomed the wall of flame. Close behind him slavering jaws were working in anticipation, and there was a strain for the last rush. There was no alternative. Straight at the fire wall where it was lowest rushed Ab, and with a great leap he went at and through the curling crest of the yellow flame!

The man had found safety! There was a moment of heat and then he knew himself to be sprawling upon green turf. A little of the strength of desperation was still with him and he bounded to his feet and looked about. There were no wolves. Beside him was a great flat rock, and he clambered upon this, and then, over the crest of the flames could see easily enough the glaring eyes of his late pursuers. They were running up and down, raging for their prey, but kept from him beyond all peradventure by the fire they could not face. Ab started upright on the rock panting and defiant, a splendid creature erect there in the firelight.

Soon there came to the man a more perfect sense of his safety. He shouted aloud to the flitting, snarling creatures, which could not harm him now; he stooped and found jagged stones, which he sent whirling among them. There was a savage satisfaction in it.

Suddenly the man fell to the ground, fairly groaning with exhaustion. Nature had become indignant and the time for recuperation had been reached. The wearied runner lay breathing heavily and was soon asleep. The flames which had afforded safety gave also a grateful warmth in the chill night, and so it was that scarcely had his body touched the ground when he became oblivious to all about him, only the heaving of the broad chest showing that the man lying fairly exposed in the light was a living thing. The varying wind sometimes carried the sheet of flame to its utmost extent toward him, so that the heat must have been intense, and again would carry it in an opposite direction while the cold air swept down upon the sleeping man. Nothing disturbed him. Inured alike to heat and cold, Ab slept on, slept for hours the sleep

which follows vast strain and endurance in a
healthy human being. Then the form lying
on the ground moved restlessly and muttered
exclamations came from the lips. The man
was dreaming.

For as the sleeper lay there—he remembered it when he awoke and wondered over it
many times in after years —Oak sprang through
the flames, as he himself had done, and soon
lay panting by his side. The lapping of the
fire, the snapping and snarling of the wolves
beyond and the familiar sound of Oak's voice
all mingled confusedly in his ears, and then
he and Oak raced together over the rough
ground, and wrestled and fought and played
as they had wrestled and fought and played
together for years. And the hours passed
and the wind changed and the flames almost
scorched him and Ab started up, looking
about him into the wild aspect of the Fire
Country; for the night had passed and the
sun had risen and set again since the exhausted
man had fallen upon the ground and become
unconscious.

Ab rolled instinctively a little away from the
smoky sheets of flame and, sitting up, looked
for Oak. He could not see him. He ran

wildly around among the rocks looking for
him and despairingly called aloud his name.
The moment his voice had been hoarsely
lifted, "Oak!" the memory of all that had
happened rushed upon him. He stood there
in the red firelight a statue of despair. Oak
was dead; he had killed Oak, and buried him
with his own hands, and yet he had seen Oak
but a minute ago! He had bounded through
the flames and had wrestled and run races
with Ab, and they had talked together, and
yet Oak must be lying in the ground back
there in the forest by the little hill. Oak was
dead. How could he get out of the ground?

Fear clutched at Ab's heart, his limbs trem-
bled under him. He whimpered like a lost
and friendless hound and crouched close to
the hospitable fire. His brain wavered under
the stress of strange new impressions. He recalled some mutterings of Old Mok about the
dead, that they had been seen after it was
known that they were deep in the ground, but
he knew it was not good to speak or think of
such things. Again Ab sprang to his feet. It
would not do to shut his eyes, for then he saw
plainly Oak in his shallow hole in the dark
earth and the face Ab had hurried to cover

first when he was burying his friend, there under the trees. And so the night wore away, sleep coming fitfully from time to time. Ab could not explore his retreat in the strange firelight nor run the risks of another night journey across the wild beasts' chosen country. He began to be hungry, with the fierce hunger of brute strength, sharpened by terrific labors, but he must wait for the morning. The night seemed endless. There was no relief from the thoughts which tortured him, but, at last, morning broke, and in action Ab found the escape he had longed for.

CHAPTER XX.

THE FIRE COUNTRY.

It was light now and the sun shone fairly on Ab's place of refuge. As his senses brought to him full appreciation he wondered at the scene about him. He was in a glade so depressed as to be a valley. About it, to the east and north and west, in a wavering, tossing wall, rose the uplifting line of fire through which he had leaped, though there were spaces where the height was insignificant. On the south, and extending till it circled a trifle to east, rose a wall of rock, evidently the end of a forest-covered promontory, for trees grew thickly to its very edge and their green branches overhung its sheer descent. Coming from some crevice of the rocks on the east, and tumbling downward through the valley, was a riotous brook, which disappeared through some opening at the west. Within this area, thus hemmed in by fire and rock, appeared no living thing save the birds which sang upon the bushes beside the small stream's banks and the butterflies which hung above the flowers and all the insect world which joined in the soft, humming chorus of the morning. It was something that Ab looked upon with delighted wonder, but without understanding. What he saw was not a marvel. It was but the result of one of many upheavals at a time when the earth's cooled shell was somewhat thinner than now and when earthquakes, though there were no cities to overthrow, at least made havoc sometimes by changing the face of nature. There had come a great semi-circular crack in the earth, near and extending to the line of the sheer rock range. The natural gas, the product of the vegetation of thousands of centuries before, had found a chance to escape and had poured forth into the outer world. Something, perhaps a lightning stroke and a flaming tree, perhaps some cave man making fire and consumed on the instant when he succeeded, had ignited the sheet of rising gas, and the result was the wall of flame. It was all natural and commonplace, for the time. There were other upleaping flame sheets in the surrounding region forever burning—as there are in northern Asia to-day—but Ab knew of these fires only from Old Mok's tales. He stood wonderstruck at what he saw about him.

But this man in the valley was young and very strong, with tissues to be renewed, and the physical man within him clamored and demanded. He must eat. He ran forward and around, anxiously observant, and soon learned that at the western end of the valley, where the little creek tumbled through a rocky cut into a lower level, there was easy exit from the fire-encompassed and protected area. He clambered along the creek's rough, descending side. He emerged upon an easier slope and then found it possible to climb the hillside to the plane of the great wood. There must, he thought, be food of some sort, even for a man with only Oak's knife in his possession! There was the forest and there were nuts. He was in the forest soon, among the gray-trunked, black-mottled beeches and the rough brown oaks. He found something of what he sought, the nuts lying under shed leaves, though the supply was scant. But nuts, to the cave man, made moderately good food, supplying a part of the sustenance he required, and Ab ate of what he could find and arose from the devouring search and looked about him.

He was weaponless, save for the knife, and a flint knife was but a thing for closest struggle. He longed now for his ax and spear and the strong bow which could hurt so at a distance. But there was one sort of weapon to be had. There was the club. He wandered about among the tops of fallen trees and wrenched at their dried limbs, and finally tore one away and broke off, later, with a prying leverage, what made a rough but available club for a cave man's purposes. It was much better than nothing. Then began a steady trot toward what should be fair life again. There were vague paths through the forest made by wild beasts. As he moved the man thought deeply.

He thought of the fire-wall, and could not with all his reasoning determine upon the cause of its existence, and so abandoned the subject as a thing, the nub of which was unreachable. That was the freshest object in his mind and the first to be mentally disposed of. But there were other subjects which came in swift succession. As he went along with a dog's gait he was not in much terror, practically weaponless as he was. His eye was good and he was going through the forest in the daylight. He was strong enough, club in hand, to meet the minor beasts. As for the others, if any of them appeared, there were the trees, and he could climb. So, as he trotted he could afford to think.

And he thought much that day, this perplexed man, our grandfather with so many "greats" before the word. He had nothing to divert him even in the selection of the course toward his cave. He noted not where the sun stood, nor in what direction the tiny headwaters of the rivulets took their course, nor how the moss grew on the trees. He traveled in the wood by instinct, by some almost unexplainable gift which comes to the thing of the woods. The wolf has it; the Indian has it; sometimes the white man of to-day has it.

As he went Ab engaged in deeper and more sustained thought than ever before in all his life. He was alone; new and strange scenes had enlarged his knowledge and swift happenings had made keener his perceptions. For days his entire being had been powerfully affected by his meeting with Lightfoot at the Feast of the Mammoth and the events which had followed that meeting in such swift succession. The tragedy of Oak's death had quickened his sensibilities. Besides, what had ensued latest had been what was required to make him in a condition for the divination of things. The wise agree that much stimulant or much deprivation enables the brain convolutions to do their work well, though deprivation gets the cleaner end. The asceticism of Marcus Aurelius was productive of greater results than the deep drinking of any gallant young Roman man of letters of whom he was a patron. The literature of fasting thinkers is something fine. Ab, after exerting his strength to the utmost for days, had not eaten of flesh, and the strong influences to which he was subjected were exerted upon a man still, practically, fasting. For a time, the rude and earth-born child of the cave was lifted into a region of comparative sentiment and imagination. It was an experience which affected materially all his later life.

Ever to the trotting man came the feelings which must follow fierce love and deadly action and vague remorse and fear of something indefinable. He saw the face and form of Lightfoot; he saw again the struggle, death-ending, with the friend of youth and of mutual growing into manhood. He remembered dimly the half insane flight, the leaps across the dreaded morass and, more distinctly, the chase by the wolves. The aspect of the Fire Country and of all that followed his awakening was, of course, yet fresh in his mind. He was burdened.

Ever uprising and oppressing above all else was the memory of the man he had killed and buried, covering the face first, so that it might not look at him. Was Oak really dead? he asked himself again! Had not he, Ab, as soon as he slept again, seen, alive and well, the close friend of his? He clung to the vision. He reasoned as deeply as it was in him to reason.

As he struggled in his mind to obtain light there came to him the fancy of other things dimly related to the death mystery which had perplexed him and all his kind. There must be some one who made the river rise and fall or the nut-bearing forest be either fruitful or the hard reverse. Who and what could it be? What should he do, what should all his friends do in the matter of relation to this unknown thing?

With this day and hour did not come really

the beginning of Ab's thought upon the subject of what was, to him and those he knew, the supernatural. He had thought in the past —he could not help it—of the shadow and the echo. He remembered how he and Oak had talked about the echo, and how they had tried to get rid of the thing which had more than once called back to them insolently across the valley. Every word they shouted this hidden creature would mockingly repeat and there was no recourse for them. They had once fully armed themselves and, in a burst of desperate bravery, had resolved to find who and what the owner of this voice was and have, at least, a fight. They had crossed the valley and ranged about the woodland whence the voice seemed to have come, but they never found what they sought!

The shadow which pursued them on sunny afternoons had puzzled them in another way. Very persistent had been the flat, black, earth-clinging and distorted thing which followed them so everywhere. What was this black, following thing, anyhow, this thing which swung its unsubstantial body around as one moved but which ever kept its own feet at the feet of the pursued, wherever there was no shade, and which lay there beside one so persistently?

But the echoes and the shadows were nothing as compared with the things which came to one at night. What were those creatures which came when a man was sleeping? Why did they escape with the dawn and appear again only when he was asleep and helpless, at least until he awoke fairly and seized his ax?

The sun rose high and dropped slowly down toward the west, where the far ocean was, and the shadows somewhat lengthened, but it was still light along the forest pathways and the untiring man still hurried on. He was now close to his country and becoming careless and at ease. But his imagination was still busy; he could not free himself of memory. There came to him still the vision of the friend he had buried, hiding his face first of all. The frenzy of his wish for knowing rushed again upon him. Where was Oak now? he demanded of himself and of all nature. "Where is Oak?" he yelled to the familiar trees beside his path. But the trees, even to the cave man, so close to them in the economy of wild life, so like them in his naturalness, could give no answer.

So the cave man struggled in his dim, uncertain way with the eternal question: "If a man die shall he live again?" So the human mind still struggles, after thousands of centuries have contributed to its development. A wall more impassable than the wall of flame Ab had so lately looked upon still rises between us and those who no longer live. We reach out for some knowledge of those who have died, and go almost into madness because we can grasp nothing. Silence unbroken, darkness impenetrable ever guard the mystery of death. In the long ages since the cave man ran that day, love and hope have in faith erected, beyond the grim barriers of blackness and despair, fair pavilions of promise and consolation, but to the stern examiners of physical fact and reality there has come no news from beyond the walls of silence since. We clamor tearfully for some word from those who are dead, but no answer comes. So Ab groped and strove alone in the forest, in his youth and ignorance, and in the youth and ignorance of our race.

Upon the pathway along the river's bank Ab emerged at last. All was familiar to him now. There, by the clump of trees in the flat below, was the place where he and Oak had dug the pit when they were but mere boys and had learned their first important lessons in sterner woodcraft.   Soon came in sight, as he ran, the entrance to the cave of his own family. He was home again.   But he was not the one who had left that rude habitation three days before.   He had gone away a youth.   He had come back one who had suffered and thought.   He came back a man.

CHAPTER XXI.

THE WOOING OF LIGHTFOOT.

LIGHTFOOT, when Ab seized Oak, had fled away from the two infuriated men, as the hare runs, and had sped into the forest. She had the impetus of new fear now and ran swiftly as became her name, never looking behind her, nor did she slacken her pace, though panting and exhausted, until she found herself approaching the cave where lived her playmate, Moonface, not more than an hour's run from her own home.

The fleeing girl was fortunate in stumbling upon her friend as soon as she came into the open space about the cave. Moonface was enjoying herself lazily that afternoon. She was leaning back idly in a swing of vines to which she had braided a flexible back, and was blinking somnolently in the sunshine as the visitor leaped from the wood. Moonface recognized her friend, gave a quavering cry of delight and came slipping and rolling recklessly to the ground to meet her. Lightfoot uttered no word. She stood breathless, and was rather carried than led by Moonface to an easy seat, moss-padded, upon twisted tree roots, which was that young lady's ordinary resting-place. Upon this seat the two sank, one overcome with past fear and present fatigue, and the other with an all-absorbing and demanding curiosity. It was beyond the ordinary scope of the self-restraining forces in Moonface to await with calm the recovery of Lightfoot's breath and powers of conversation. She pinched and shook her friend and demanded, half-crying but impatiently, some explanation. It was a great hour for Moonface, the greatest in her life. Here was her friend and dictator panting and terrified like some weak, hunted-down thing of the wood. It was a marvel. At last Lightfoot spoke:

"They are fighting at the foot of the hill!" she said, and Moonface at once guessed the whole story, for she was not blind, this wide-mouthed creature.

"Why did you run away?" she asked.

"I ran because I was scared. One of them must be dead before this time. I am glad I am alive myself," Lightfoot gasped. Then the girl covered her face with her hands as she recalled Ab's face, distorted by passion and murderous hate, and Oak's equally maddened look as, before the onrush, he had grasped her so firmly that the marks of his fingers remained blue upon her arms and slender waist and neck.

Then Lightfoot, slow to regain her composure, told tremblingly the story of all that had occurred, finding comfort in the unaffrighted look upon the face, as well as in the reassuring talk, of her easy-going, unimaginative and cheerful and faithful companion. She remained as a guest at the cave overnight and the next forenoon, when she took her way for home, she was accompanied by Moonface. Gradually, as the hours passed, Lightfoot regained something of her usual frame of mind and a little of her ordinary manner of careless light-heartedness, but when home had been reached and the girls had rested and eaten and she heard Moonface telling anew for her the story of the flight in the wood, while her father, Hilltop, and her two strapping brothers listened with interest, but with no degree of excitement, she felt again the wild alarm and horror and uncertainty which had affected her when first she fled from what was to her so

dreadful.   She crept away from the cave door
near which the others sat enjoying the balmy
midsummer afternoon, beckoning to one of
her brothers to follow her, as the big fellow
did unquestioningly, for Lightfoot had been,
almost from young girlhood, the dominant
force in the family, even the strong father,
though it was contrary to the spirit of the
time, admiring and yielding to his one daughter without   much   comment.   The great,
hulking youth, well armed and ready for any
adventure, joined her, nothing loth, and the
two disappeared, like shadows, in the depths
of the forest.

Lightfoot had been the housekeeper in the
cave of Hilltop, the cave of the greatest hunter of the region, young despite the years
which had encompassed him, and father of two
boys who were fine specimens of the better
men of the time.   They were splendid whelps,
and this slim thing, whom they had cared for
as she grew, dominated them easily, though
the age was not one of vast family affection,
while chivalry, of course, did not exist.   Hilltop's wife had died two years before, and
Lightfoot, with unconscious force, had taken
her mother's place.   There was none other

with woman's ways to help the men in the
rock-guarded home on the windy hill.   Hilltop
had not been altogether unthinking all this
time.   He had often looked upon his daughter's friend, the jolly, swart and well-fed Moonface, and had much approved of her, but, to-
day, as he listened to her story, he did not pay
such attention as was demanded by the interest of the theme.   An occasional death, though
it were the killing of one cave man by another,
was not a matter of huge importance.   He
was not inflamed in any way by what he heard,
but as he looked and listened to the comfortable young person who was speaking, the idea,
hastened it may be by some loving and domestic instinct, grew slowly in his brain that
she might make for him as excellent a mate as
any other of the "good matches" to be found
in the immediately surrounding country.   He
was a most directly reasoning person, this
Hilltop, best of hunters and generally respected on the forest ridges.   After the thought
once dawned upon him, it grew and grew, and
an idea fairly developed in Hilltop's mind
meant action.   His fifty-five years of age had
hardly cooled and had certainly not nearly
approached to freezing the blood in his out-

standing veins. He had a suit to make, and make at once. That he might have no interruption he bade Stone-Arm, his remaining son, who sat on a rock near by, and who had listened, open-mouthed, to the recital of Moonface, to seek his brother and Lightfoot in the forest path. There might be beasts abroad and two men were better than one, said this crafty father-hunter-lover.

The boy, clever tracker as a red Indian or Australian trailer, soon found the path his brother and Lightfoot had taken and joined them. As he listened to what they were saying he was glad he had been sent to follow them. They were hastening toward the valley. The trees were beginning to cast long shadows when the three came to where the more abrupt hillside reached the slope and where the torn ground, broken limbs and twigs and deep-indented footprints in the soil gave glaring evidence to the eye of yesterday's struggle. But, aside from all this, there was something else. There was a carpet of yellowish-brown leaves, at the edge of the circle of fray, where a man had fallen. On the clean stretch of evenly rain-packed leaves there were spots from which the scarlet had but lately faded into crimson. There was a place where the surface was disturbed and sunken a little. All three knew that a man had died there.

The two young men and their sister stood together uttering no word. The men were amazed. The woman half comprehended all. She did not hesitate a moment. Guided by a sure instinct, Lightfoot reached, without thought or conscious search, the spot of un-natural earth which reared itself so near to them, the spot where was fresh stone-covered soil and where a man was buried. The pile of stones, newly heaped upon the moist earth, told their story.

Someone was buried there, but whom? Was it Oak or Ab?

"Shall I dig?" said Stone-Arm, making ready for the task, while Branch, his elder brother, prepared for work as well.

"No! No!" cried Lightfoot. "He is buried deep and the stones are over him. It will be night soon and the wolves and hyenas would be here before we could get away. Let it be. Someone is there, but the one who killed him has buried him. He will come back!" The two boys were silent, and Lightfoot led the way toward home.

When the three reached the cave of Hilltop
the sun was setting. Something had happened at the cave, but there arises at this
point no stern demand for going into details.
Hilltop, brave man, was no laggard in wooing,
and Moonface was not a nervous young person.
When the other members of the household
reached the cave Moonface was already in-
stalled as mistress. There would be no repri-
sals from an injured family. The girl had
lived with her ancient father, whom she had
half-supported and who would, possibly, be
transplanted to Hilltop's cave for such potter-
ing life as he was still capable of during the
rest of his existence. The new régime was
fairly established.

The arrangement suited Lightfoot well
enough. This astounding stepmother had
been her humble but faithful friend. Lightfoot was a ruling woman spirit wherever she
was, and she knew it, though she bowed at all
times to the rule of strength as the only law.
Nevertheless she knew how to get her own
way. With Moonface, everything was easy
for her and she found it rather pleasant than
otherwise to find the other young woman made
suddenly a permanent resident of the cave in

which she had been born and had lived all her life.   As the two girls met, and the situation was curtly announced by Hilltop, their faces were worth the seeing.   There was alarm and hopefulness upon the countenance of Moon-face, sudden astonishment and indignation, and then reflection, upon the face of Light-foot.   After a few moments of thought both girls laughed cheerfully.

The story of the newly found grave made but little impression upon the group and Light-foot, the only one of the household who thought much about it, thought silently.   To her the single question was: ''Who lay there?''   There was nothing strange to the others of the family in the thought that one man should have killed another, and no one attached blame to or pro-posed punishment of the slayer.   Sometimes after such a happening, the cave man who had slain another might have a rock rolled sud-denly upon him from a height, or in passing a thicket have the flint head of a spear driven through him, but this was only the deed, per-haps, of an enraged father or brother, not in any sense a matter of course in the way of jus-tice, and even such attempt at reprisal was not the rule.

But in the bosom of Lightfoot was a weight like a stone. It was as heavy, she thought, as one of the stones on the bare ground over the body of the man who lay there in the dark earth, because he had run after her. Who was it? It might be Ab! And all through the night the girl tossed uneasily on her bed of leaves, as she did for nights to come.

As for Moonface, who shall say what that rotund and hairy young person thought when the family had settled down to the changed order of things and she had adjusted herself to the duties of a matron in her new home? She was not less broadly buoyant and beaming, but who can tell that, when she noted Lightfoot's burning look and thoughtful mien, Moonface did not sometimes think of the two young men who, but yesterday, had rejoiced in such strength and vigor and charm of power and who were so good to look upon? She was a wife now, but to another sort of man. Even the feminine among writers of erotic novels have not yet revealed what the young moon thinks when she "holds the old moon in her arms." Anyhow, Hilltop was a defense and a great provider of food. He was a fine figure of a man, too.

Lightfoot was not much in the cave now. She lingered about the open space or wandered in the near wood. A woman's instinct told her to be out-doors all the time she could. A man would seek her, but with the thought came an awful dread. Which man? One afternoon she saw something.

Two gray forms flitted across an open space in the forest near the cave, and in a moment the girl was in a treetop. What followed was the unexpected. Close behind the gray things came a man, fully armed, straight, eager and alert and silent in his wood surroundings, with eyes roving over and searching all the open space about the cave of Hilltop. The man was Ab.

The girl gave a shriek of delight, then, alarmed at the sound she had made, cowered behind a refuge of leaves and branches. She was happy beyond all her experience before. The question which had been in all her thoughts was answered! It was Oak, not Ab, who lay in the ground on the hillside. And, even as she realized this fully, there was a swift upward scramble and the young cave man was beside her on the limb. There was no running away this time. The girl's face told

its story well enough, so well that Ab, still
lately doubting, though resolved, knew that
his fitting mate belonged to him.   There came
to them the happiness which ever comes to
lovers, be they man or bird or beast, and then
came swift conclusion.   He told her she must
go with him at once, told her of the new cave
and of all he had done, but the girl, well aware
of the dangers of the beast-haunted region
where the new home had been selected, was
thoroughly alarmed.   Then Ab told her of the
little flying spears which Old Mok had made
for him, and about the wonderful bow which
sent them to their mark, and the girl was reassured and soon began to feel exceedingly
brave and proud of her lover and his prowess.

No need of carrying off a girl by force or
craft on this occasion, for Hilltop had fully
recognized Ab's strength and quality.   The
two went to the cave together and there was
eating and then, later, two skin-clad human
beings, a man and a woman, went away together through the forest.   Their journey was
a long one and a careful lookout was necessary
as they hurried along a pathway of the strange
country.   But the cave was reached at last,

just as the sun burned red and gave a rosy glow to everything.

Silently the two came into the open space in front of what was to be their fortress and abode. Solid was the rock about the entrance and narrow the blocked opening. Smoke curled in a pretty spiral upward from where smoldered the fire Ab had made the day before. Lightfoot looked upon it all and laughed joyously, though tremblingly, for she had now given herself to a man and he had brought her to his place of living.

As for the man, he looked down upon the girl delightedly. His pulse beat fast. He put his arm about her and together they entered the cave. There was a marriage but no ceremony. Just as robins mate when they have met or as the buck and doe, so faithful man and wife became these two.

Darkness fell, the fire at the cave entrance flashed up fiercely and Ab and Lightfoot were "at home."

CHAPTER XXII.

THE HONEYMOON.

THE sun shone brilliantly, birds were singing and the balsam firs gave forth their morning incense as Ab and Lightfoot issued from
their cave. They had eaten heartily, and
came out buoyant and delighted with the
world which was theirs. The chattering of
the waterfowl along the river reached their
ears faintly, the leaves were moved by a gentle
breeze, there was a hum of insects in the air
and the very pulse of living could be felt. Ab
carried his new weapon proudly, hungering
for the love and admiration of this girl of his,
and eager to show her its powers and to exhibit his own skill. At his back hung his
quiver of mammoth bone. His bow, un-
strung, was in his hand. In front of the cave
was a bare area of many yards in extent,
then came a few scattering trees and, at a
distance of perhaps two hundred yards, the
forest began. Across the open space of
ground, with its great mass of branches

crushed together not far from the cave's mouth, had fallen one of the gigantic conifers of the time, and was there gradually decaying, its huge limbs and bole, disintegrating, and dry as punk, affording, close at hand, a vast fuel supply, the exceptional value of which Ab had recognized when making his selection of a home. Near the edge of the little clearing made by nature, Ab seated himself upon a log, and drawing Lightfoot down to a seat beside him, began enthusiastically to make clear the marvels of the weapon he had devised and which he and Old Mok had developed into something startling in its possibilities.

All details of the explanation made by the earnest young hunter, it is probable, Lightfoot did not comprehend. She looked proudly at him, fingering the flint pointed arrows curiously, yet seemed rather intent upon the man than the wood and stone. But when he pointed at a great knot in a tree near them and bent his bow and sent an arrow fairly into the target, and when, even with her strength, Lightfoot could not pull the arrow out, she was wild with admiration and excitement. She begged to be taught how to use, herself, this wonderful new weapon, for she recognized as readily as could anyone its adaptation to the use of one of inferior strength. The delighted lover was certainly as desirous as she that she should some day become an expert. He handed her the bow, retaining, slung over his shoulder, fortunately, as it developed, the bone quiver full of Old Mok's best arrows. He taught her, first, how to bend and string the bow. There were failures and successes, and there was much laughter from the merry-hearted Lightfoot. Finally, it happened that Ab was not just content with the quality of the particular arrow which he had selected for Lightfoot's use. He had taken a slender one with a clean flint head, but something about the notch had not quite suited him. With a thin, hard stone scraper, carried in a pouch of his furry garb, he began rasping and filing at this notch to make it better fit the string of tendons, while Lightfoot, with the bow still strung, stood beside him. At last, tired of holding the thing in her hands, she passed it over her head and one shoulder and stood there jauntily, with both hands free, while the man scraped away with the one little flake of flint in his possession, and, as he worked, paused from time to time to note how well he was rounding the notch in the end of the slight hardwood shaft. It was just as he was holding up to her eyes the arrow, now made almost an ideal one, according to his fancy, when there came to the ears of the two a sound, distinct, ominous and implying to them deadly peril, a sound such that, though nerves spoke and muscles acted, they were very near the momentary paralysis which sometimes come from sudden fearful shock. From close beside them came the half grunt and half growl of the great cave bear!

With the instinct born of generations, each leaped independently toward the nearest tree, and, with the unconscious strength and celerity which comes to even wild animals with the dread of death at hand, each clambered to a treetop before a word was spoken. Scarcely had either left the ground before there was a rush into the open glade of a huge brown hairy form, and this was instantly followed by another. As Ab and Lightfoot climbed far amid the branches and looked down, they saw upreared at the base of each tree the figure of one of the monsters whose hungry exclamations they knew so well. They had been careless, these two lovers, especially the man.

He had known well, but for the moment had forgotten how beast-infested was the immediate area about his new home, and now had come the consequence of his thoughtlessness. He and his wife had been driven to the tree-tops within a few yards of their own hearth-stone, leaving their weapons inside their cave!

Alarmed and panting, after settling down to a firm seat far aloft, each looked about to see what had become of the other. Each was at once reassured as to the present, and each became much perplexed as to the future. The cave bear, like his weaker and degenerate descendant, the grizzly of to-day, had the quality of persistence well developed, and both Ab and Lightfoot knew that the seige of their enemies would be something more than for the moment. The trees in which they perched were very close to the wood, but not so close that the forest could be reached by passing from branch to branch. Their two trees were not far from each other, but their branches did not intermingle. There was a distinct opening between them. The tree up which Lightfoot had scrambled was a great fir towering high above the strong beech in which Ab had found his safety. Branches of the fir hung down until between their ends and Ab's less lofty covert there were but a few yards of space. Still, one trying to reach the beech from the lofty fir would find an unpleasantly wide gap.

Each of the creatures in the tree was unarmed. Ab still bore the quiver full of admirable arrows, and across the breast of Lightfoot still hung the strong bow which she had slung about her in such blithesome mood. Soon began an exceedingly earnest conversation. Ab, eager to reach again the fair creature who now belonged to him, was half frantic with rage, and Lightfoot was far from her usual mood of careless gaiety. The two talked and considered, though but to little purpose, and, finally, after weary hours, the night came on. It was a trying situation. Man and woman were in equal danger. The bears were hungry —and the cave bear knew his quarry. The beasts beneath were not disposed to leave the prey they had imprisoned aloft. The night grew, but either Ab or Lightfoot, looking down, could see the glare of small, hungry eyes. There was gentle talk between the two, for this was a great strait and, in straits, souls, be they prehistoric, historic or of to-day,

always come closer together. Very much
more loving lovers, even, than they were before, became the two perched aloft that night.
It was a comfort for the wedded pair to call to
each other through the darkness. After a
time, however, muscles grew lax with the continued strain. Weariness clouded the spirits
of the couple and almost overcame them and
only the thing which has always, in great stress,
given the greatest strength in this world—the
love of male and female—sustained them.
They stood the test pretty well. To sleep in
a tree top was an easy thing for them, with
the precautions, simple and natural, of the
time. Each plaited a withe of twigs with
which to be tied to the tree or limb, and resting in the hollow nest where some great limb
joined the bole, slept as sleep tired children,
until the awakening of nature awoke these
who were nature's own. When Ab awoke, he
had more on his mind than Lightfoot, for he
was the one who must care for the two. He
blinked and wondered where he was. Then
he remembered all, suddenly. He looked
across anxiously at a slender brown thing
lying asleep, coiled so close to the bole of the
tree to which she was bound that she seemed

almost a part of it. Then he looked down, and, after what he saw, thought very seriously. The bears were there! He looked up at the bright sky and all about him, and inhaled all the fragrance of the forest, and felt strong, and that he knew what he should do. He called aloud.

The girl awoke, frightened. She would have fallen had she not been bound to the tree. Gradually, the full meaning of the situation dawned upon her and she began to cry. She was hungry, her limbs were stiffened by her bands, and there was death below. But there, close to her, was the Man. His voice gradually reassured her. He was becoming angry now, almost raging. Here he was, the lord of a cave, independent and master as much as any other man whom he knew, perched in one tree while his bride of a day was in the top of another, yet kept apart from her by the brutes below!

He had decided what to do, and now he talked to Lightfoot with all the frankness of the strong male who felt that he had another to care for, and who realized his responsibility and authority together. As the strength and decided personality of the young man came to her through his voice, the young woman drew her scanty fur robe about her and checked her tears. She became comparatively calm and reasonable.

The tree in which Lightfoot had found refuge had many long slender branches lowering toward the giant beech into which the man had made his retreat. Ab argued that it was possible—barely possible—for Lightfoot's compact, agile, slender body to be launched in just the right way from one of the branches of the taller tree, and, swinging in its descent across the space between the two, lodge among the branches of the beech with him. Strong arms ready to clasp her as she came and to withstand the shock and to hold her safely he promised and, to enforce his plea, he pointed out that, unless they thus took their fate in hand, there was starvation awaiting them as they were, while carrying out his plan, if any accident befell, there was only swift though dreadful death to reckon with. There was one chance for their lives and that chance must be taken. Ab called to his young wife:

"Crawl out upon a branch above me, swing down from it, swing hard and throw yourself

to me.   I will catch you and hold you.   I am
strong."

The woman, with all faith in the man, still
demurred.   It was a great test, even for the
times and the occasion.   But hunger was upon
her and she was cold and was, naturally, very
brave.   She lowered herself and climbed down
and reached an out-extending limb, and there,
across the gap, she saw Ab with his strong legs
twined about the uprearing branch along which
he laid, with giant brown arms stretched out
confidently and with eyes steadily regarding
her, eyes which had love and longing and a
lot of fight in them.   She walked out along
the limb, holding herself safely by a firm hand-
hold on the limb above, until the one her bare
feet rested upon swayed and tipped uncertainly.   Then came her time of trial of nerve
and trust.   Suddenly she stooped, caught the
lower limb with her hands and then swung
beneath it, hanging by her hands alone, and,
hand over hand, passed herself along until she
reached almost its end.   Then she began
swaying back and forth.   She was but a few
yards above Ab now, dangling in mid-air,
while, below her, the two hungry bears had
rushed together and were looking upward with

red, anticipating eyes, the ooze coming from their mouths. The moment was awful. Soon she must be a mangled thing devoured by frightful beasts, or else a woman with a life renewed. She looked at Ab, and, with courage regained, prepared for the great effort which must end all or gain a better lease of life.

She swung back and forth, each drawing up and outreach and flexible motion of her arms giving more momentum to the sway and conserving force for the launch of herself she was about to make. The desperation and strength of a wood-wise creature, so bravely combined, alone enabled her to obey Ab's hoarse command.

Ab, with his arms outreaching in their strength, feeling the fierce eyes of the hungry bears below boring into his very heart, leaned forward and upward as the swing of the woman reached its climax. With a cry of warning, the woman launched herself and shot downward and forward, like a bolt to its mark, a very desirable lump of femininity as appearing in mid-air, but one somewhat forcible in its alighting.

Ab was strong, but when that girl landed fairly in his brawny arms, as she did beauti-

fully, it was touch and go, for a fraction of a
second, whether both should fall to the ground
together or both be saved. He caught her
deftly, but there was a great shock and swing
and then, with a vast effort, there came recovery and the man drew himself, shaking,
back to the support of the branch from which
he had been almost wrenched away, at the
same time placing beside him the object he
had just caught.

There was absolute silence for a moment or
two between these unconventional lovers to
whom had come escape from a hard situation.
They were drawing deep breaths and recover-
ing an equilibrium. There they sat together
on the strong branch, each of them as secure
and, for the moment, as perfectly at home as
if lying on a couch in the cave. Each of them
was panting and each of them rejoicing. It
was unlikely that upon their trained, robust
nerves the life-endangering episode of a moment could have a more than passing effect.
They sat so together for some minutes with
arms entwined, still drawing deep breaths,
and, a little later, began to laugh chucklingly,
as breath came to be spared for such exhibition of human feeling. Gradually, the in-

drawing and expelling of the glorious air shortened. The two had regained their normal condition and Ab's face lengthened and the lines upon it became more distinct. He was all himself again, but in no dallying mood. He gave a triumphant whoop which echoed through the forest, shook his clenched hand savagely at the brutes below and reached toward Lightfoot for the bow which hung about her shoulders.

CHAPTER XXIII.

MORE OF THE HONEYMOON.

THE brown, downy woman knew, on the instant, what was her husband's mood and immediate intent when he thus shouted and took into his own keeping again the stiff bow which hung about her shoulders. She knew that her lord was not merely in a glad, but that he was also in a vengeful frame of mind, that he wanted from her what would enable him to kill things, and that, equipped again, he was full of the spirit of fight. She knew that, of the four animals grouped together, two huge creatures of the ground and two slighter ones perched in a tree top, the chances were that the condition of those below had suddenly become the less preferable.

The bow was about Ab's shoulders instantly, and then this preposterous young gentleman of the period turned to the woman and laughed, and caught her in one of his arms a little closer, and drew her up against him and laid his cheek against her own for a moment and drew it

away and laughed again. The kiss, it is be-
lieved, had not fully developed itself in the
cave man's time, but there were substitutes.
Then, releasing her, he said gleefully and
chuckingly, ''follow me;'' and they clambered
down the bole of the beech together until they
reached the biggest and very lowest limb of
all. It was perhaps twenty feet above the
ground. A little below their dangling feet the
hungry bears, hitherto more patient, now,
with their expected prey so close at hand, becoming desperately excited, ran about, frothing
and foaming and red-eyed, uprearing themselves in awful nearness, at times, in their
eagerness to reach the prey which they had so
awaited and which, to their intelligence,
seemed about falling into their jaws. They
had so driven into trees before, and finally
consumed exhausted cave men and women.
As bears went, they were doubtless logical
animals. They could not know that there
had come into possession of this particular
pair of creatures of the sort they had occasionally eaten, a trifling thing of wood and sinew
string and flint point, which was destined
henceforth to make a decided change in the
relative condition of the biped and quadruped

hunters of the time.   How could they know
that something small and sharp would fly
down and sting them more deeply than they
had ever been stung before, that it would
sting so deeply that their arteries might
be cut, or their hearts pierced and that
then they must lie down and die?   The well-
thrown spear had been, in other ages, a vast
surprise to the carnivora of the period, but
there was something yet to learn.

When they had reached the huge branch
so near the ground both Ab and Lightfoot
were for a moment startled and lifted their
feet instinctively, but it was only for a moment
in the case of the man.   He knew that he
was perfectly safe and that he had with him
an engine of death.   He selected his best and
strongest arrow, he fitted it carefully to the
string and then, as his mother had done years
before above the hyena which sought her
child, he reached one foot down as far as
he could, and swung it back and forth tan-
talizingly, just above the larger of the hungry
beasts below.   The monster, fierce with hunger and the desire for prey, roared aloud and
upreared himself by the tree trunk and tore
the bark with his strong claws, throwing back

his great head as he looked upward at the
quarry so near him and yet just beyond his
reach.   This was the man's opportunity.   Ab
drew back the arrow till the flint head rested
close by his out-straining hand and the tough
wood of the bow creaked under the thrust of
his muscled arm.   Then he released the shaft.
So close together were man and bear that
archer's skill of aim was not required.   The
brown target could not be missed.   The arrow
struck with a tear and the flint head drove
through skin and tissue till its point protruded
at the back of the great brute's neck.   The
bear fell suddenly backward, then rose again
and reached blindly at its neck with its huge
fore-paws, while from where the arrow had
entered the blood came out in spurts.   Suddenly the bear ceased its appalling roars and
started for the cave.   There had come to it
the instinct which makes such great beasts
seek to die alone.   It rushed at the narrow
entrance but its course was scarcely noted by
the couple in the tree.   The other bear, the
female, was seeking to reach them in no less
savage mood than had animated her stricken
mate.

Not often, when the cave man first learned

the use of the bow, came to him such fortune
with a first strong shot as that which had so
come to Ab.   Again he selected a good arrow,
again shot his strongest and best, but the
shaft only buried itself in the shoulder and
served but to drive to absolute madness the
raging creature thus sorely hurt.   The forest echoed with the roaring of the infuriated
animal, and as she reared herself clambering
against the tree the tough fiber was rended
away in great slivers, and the man and woman
were glad that the trunk was thick and that
they owned a natural citadel.   Again and
again did Ab discharge his arrows and still fail
to reach a vital part of the terror below.   She
fairly bristled with the shafts.   It was inevitable that she must die, but when the last shot
had sped she was still infuriate and, apparently, as strong as ever.   The archer looked
down upon her with some measure of de-
spondency in his face, but by no means with
despair.   He and his bride must wait.   That
was all, and this he told to Lightfoot.   That
intelligent and reliable young helpmate of a
few hours, who had looked upon what had
occurred with an awed admiration, did not
exhibit any depression.   Her husband, fortu-

nate Benedict, had produced a great effect upon her by his feat. She felt herself something like a queen. Had she known enough and had the fancies of the Ruth of some thousands of decades later she would have told him how completely thenceforth his people were her people and his gods her gods.

The she bear became finally somewhat quieted; she tore less angrily at the tree and made less of the terrible clamor which had for the moment driven from the immediate region all the inmates of the wood, for none save the cave tiger cared to be in the immediate neighborhood of the cave bear. Her roars changed into roaring growls, and she wandered staggeringly about. At last she started blindly and weakly toward the forest, and just as she had passed beneath its shadow, paused, weaved back and forth for a moment, and then fell over heavily. She was dead.

Not an action of the beast had escaped the eyes of Ab. Well he knew the ways of wounded things. As the bear toppled over he gave utterance to a whoop and, with a word to the girl beside him, slid lightly to the ground, she following him at once. It was very good to be upon the earth again. Ab

stamped with his feet and stretched his arms,
and the woman danced upon the grass and
laughed gleefully.   But this was only for a
moment or so.   Ab started toward the cave,
and as he reached the entrance, gave a great
cry of rage and dismay.   Lightfoot ran to his
side and even her ready laugh failed her when
she looked upon his perplexed and stormy
countenance and saw what had happened.
The rump of the monster he bear was what
she looked upon.   The beast, in his instinctive
effort to crawl into some dark place to die,
had fairly driven himself into the cave's entrance, dislodging some of the stones Ab had
placed there, had wedged himself in firmly,
and had died before he could extricate his
great carcass.   The two human beings were
homeless and, with all the arrows gone,
weaponless, in the midst of a region so
dangerously infested that any movement afoot
was but inviting death.   They were hungry,
too, for many hours had passed since they
had tasted food.   It was not matter of surprise that even the stout-hearted cave man
stood aghast.

The occasion for Ab's alarm was fully veri-
fied.   From the spot where the cave bear lay

at the forest's edge came a sharp, snapping growl. The lurking hyenas had found the food, and a long, inquiring howl from another direction told that the wolves had scented it and were gathering. For the instant Ab was himself almost helpless with fear. The woman was simply nerveless. Then the man, so accustomed to physical danger, recovered himself. He sprang forward, seized a stout fragment of limb which might serve as a sort of weapon, and, turning to the woman, said only the one word "fire."

Lightfoot understood and life came to her again. None in all the region could make a fire more swiftly than she. Her quick eye detected just the base she wanted in a punkish fragment of wood and the harder and pointed bit of limb to be used in making the friction. In a time scarcely worth the noting the point was whirling about and burning into the wooden base, twirling with a skill and velocity not comprehensible by us to-day, for the cave people had perfected wonderfully this greatest manual art of the time, and Lightfoot, muscular and enduring, was, as already said, in this thing the cleverest among the clever. Ab, with ready club in hand, advanced cautiously toward the point at the wood's edge where lay the body of the bear. He paused as he came near enough to see what was happening. Four great hyenas were tearing eagerly at the flesh of the dead brute, and behind them, deeper in the wood, were shining eyes, and Ab knew that the wolf pack was gathering. The bear consumed, the man and woman, without defense, would surely be devoured. It was a desperate strait, but, though he was weaponless, there was the cave man's great resort, the fire, and there might be a chance for life. To seek the tree tops would be dangerous even now, and once ensconced in such harborage, only starvation was awaiting. He moved back noiselessly, with as little apparent motion as possible, for he did not want to attract the attention of the gleaming eyes in the distance, until he came near Lightfoot again, and then he abandoned caution of movement and began tearing frantically at the limbs and débris of the great dead conifer, and to build a semicircular fence in front of the cave entrance. He did the swift work of half a score of men in his desperation and anxiety, his great strength serving him well in his compelling strait.

Meanwhile the stick twirled and rasped in the hands of the brown woman seated on the ground, and at last a tiny thread of smoke arose. The continued friction had done its work. Deft himself at fire-making, Ab knew just what was wanted at this moment and ran to his wife's side with punk from the dead tree, rubbed to a powder in his hard hands. The powder, poured gently down upon the point where the increasing heat had brought the gleam of fire, burst, almost at once, into a little flame. What followed was simple and easy. Dry twigs made the slight flame a greater one and then, at a dozen different points, the wall which Ab had built was fired. They were safe, for the time at least. Behind them was the uprearing rock in which was the cave and before them, almost encircling them completely, was the ring of fire which no wild beast would cross. At one end, close to the rock, a space had been left by Ab, that he and Lightfoot might, through it, reach the vast store of fuel which lay there ready to the hand and so close that there was no danger in visiting it. Hardly had the flame extended itself along the slight wooden barrier than the whole wood and clearing resounded with terrifying sounds. The wolf pack had increased until strong enough to battle with the hyenas for the remainder of the feast in the wood, and their fight was on.

The feeling of terror had passed away from this young bride and groom, with the assurance of present safety, and Ab felt the need of eating. "There is meat," he said, as he pointed toward the haunches of the bear, half-protruding from the rock, "and there is fire. The fire will cook the meat, and, besides, we are safe. We will eat!"

The bridegroom of but a day or two said this somewhat grandiloquently, but he was not disposed to be vain or grandiloquent a little later. He put his hand to the belt of his furry garb and found no sharp flint knife there! It had been lost in his late tree clambering. He put his hand into the pouch of his cloak and found only the flint skin scraper, the scraper with which he had improved the arrow's notch, though it was not originally intended for such use. It was all that remained to him of weapon or utensil. But it would cut or tear, though with infinite effort, and the man, to re-assure the woman, laughed, and assailed the brown haunch before him. Even with his strength, it was difficult for Ab to penetrate the tough skin of the bear with an implement intended for scraping, not for cutting, and it was only after he had finally cut, or rather dug, away enough to enable him to get his fingers under the skin and tear away an area of it by sheer main strength that the flesh was made available. That end once attained, there followed a hard transverse digging with the scraper, a grasp about tissue of strong, impressed fingers, and a shred of flesh came away. It was tossed at once to a young person who, long twig in hand, stood eagerly waiting. She caught the shred as she had caught the fine bit of mammoth when first she and Ab had met, and it was at once impaled and thrust into the flames. It was withdrawn, it is to be feared, a trifle underdone, and then it disappeared, as did other shreds of excellent bear's meat which came following. It was a sight for a dyspeptic to note the eating of this belle-matron of the region on this somewhat exceptional occasion.

Strip after strip did Ab tear away and toss to his wife until the expression on her face became a shade more peaceful and then it dawned upon him that she was eating and that he was not.   There was clamor in his stomach. He sprang away from the bear, gave Lightfoot the scraper and commanded her to get food for him as he had done for her.   The girl complied and did as well as had done the man in digging away the meat. He ate as she had done, and, at last, partly gorged and content, allowed her to take her place at the fire and again eat to his serving.   He had shown what, from the standard of the time, must be counted as most gallant and generous and courteous demeanor.   He had thought a little of the woman.

A tiny rill of cold water trickled down on one side of the outer door of their cave. With this their thirst was slaked, and they ate and ate.   The shadows lengthened and Ab replenished again and again the fire.   From the semicircle of forest all about came the sound of footsteps rustling in the leaves.   But the two people inside the fire fence, hungry no longer, were content.   Ab talked to his wife:

"The fire will keep the man-eating things away," he said.   "I ran not long ago with things behind me, and I would have been eaten had I not come upon a ring of fire like the one we have made.   I leaped it and the eaters could not reach me. But, for the fire I leaped there was no wood. It came out of a crack in the ground. Some day we will go there and I will show you that thing which is so strange."

The woman listened, delighted, but, at last, there was a nodding of the head. She lay back upon the grass a sleepy being. Ab looked at her and thought deeply. Where was safety? As they were, one of them must be awake all the time to keep the fire replenished. Until he could enter the cave again he must be weaponless. Only the fire could protect the two. They had heat and food and nothing to fear for the moment, but they must fairly eat their way into a safety which would be permanent!

He kept the fire alight far into the darkness, and then, piling the fuel high all along the line of defense, he aroused the sleeping woman and told her she must keep the flames bright while he slept in his turn. She was just the wife for such an emergency as this, and rose uncomplainingly to do her part of the guarding work. From the forest all about came snarling sounds or threatening growls, and eyes blazed in the somber depths beneath the trees.

There were hungry things out there and they wanted to eat a man and woman, but fire they feared.   The woman was not afraid.

After hours had passed the man awoke and took the woman's place and she slept in his stead.   Morning came and the sounds from the forest died away partly, but the man and woman knew of the fierce creatures still lurking there.   They knew what was before them. They must delve and eat their way into the cave as soon as possible.

Ab scraped at the bear's huge body with his inefficient bit of flint and dug away food in abundance, which he heaped up in a little red mound inside the fire, but the bear was a monstrous beast and it was a long way from tail to head.   The days of the honeymoon passed with a degree of travail, for there was no moment when one of the two must not be awake feeding the guarding fire or digging at the bear.   They ate still heartily on the second day but it is simple, truthful history to admit that on the sixth day bear's meat palled somewhat on the happy couple.   To have eaten thirty quails in thirty days or, at a pinch, thirty quails in two days would have been nothing to either of them, but bear's meat eaten as part of what might be called a tunneling exploit ceased, finally, to possess an attractive flavor. There was a degree of shade cast by all these obtrusive circumstances across this honeymoon, but there came a day and hour when the bear was largely eaten, and fairly dug away as to much of the rest of him, and then, quite suddenly, his head and fore-quarters toppled forward into the cave, leaving the passage free, and when Ab and Lightfoot followed, one shouting and the other laughing, one coming again to his fortress and his weapons and his power, and the other to her hearth and duties.

CHAPTER XXIV.

THE FIRE COUNTRY AGAIN.

THE sun rose brightly the next morning and when Ab, armed and watchful, rolled the big stone away and passed the smoldering fire and issued from the cave into the open, the scene he looked upon was fair in every way. Of what had been left of the great bear not a trace remained. Even the bones had been dragged into the forest by the ravening creatures who had fed there during the night. There were birds singing and there were no enemies in sight. Ab called to Lightfoot and the two went forth together, loving and brave, but no longer careless in that too interesting region.

And so began the home life of these two people. It was, in its way and relatively, as sweet and delicious as the first home life of any loving and appreciating man and woman of to-day. The two were very close, as the conditions under which they lived demanded. They were the only human beings within a radius of miles. The family of the cave man of the time was serenely independent, each having its own territory, and depending upon itself for its existence. And the two troubled themselves about nothing. Who better than they could daily win the means of animal subsistence?

Ab taught Lightfoot the art of cracking away the flakes of the flint nodules and of the finer chipping and rasping which made perfect the spear and arrowheads, and never was pupil swifter in the learning. He taught her, too, the use of his new weapon, and in all his life he did no wiser thing! It was not long before she became easily his superior with the bow, so far as her strength would allow, and her strength was far from insignificant. Her arrows flew with greater accuracy than his, though the buzzing shaft had not as yet, and did not have for many centuries later, the "gray goose" feather which made the doing of its mission far more certain. Lightfoot brought to the cave the capercailzie and willow grouse and other birds which were good things for the larder, and Ab looked on admiringly. Even in their joint hunting, when there was a half rivalry, he was happy in her. Somehow, the arrow sang more merrily when it flew from Lightfoot's bow.

Better than Ab, too, could the young wife do rare climbing when in a nest far out upon some branch were eggs good for roasting and which could be reached only by a light-weight. And she learned the woods about them well, and, though ever dreading when alone, found where were the trees from which fell the greatest store of nuts and where, in the mud along the river's side, her long and highly educated toes could reach the clams which were excellent to feed upon.

But never did the hunter leave the cave without a fear. Ever, even in the daytime, was there too much rustling among the leaves of the near forest. Ever when day had gone was there the sound of padded feet on the sward about the cave's blocked entrance. Ever, at night, looking out through the narrow space between the heaped rocks, could the two inside the cave see fierce and blazing eyes and there would come to them the sound of snarls and growls as the beasts of different quality met one another. Yet the two cared little for these fearful surroundings of the darkness. They were safe enough. In the morning there were no signs of the lurking beasts of prey. They were somewhere near, though, and waiting, and so Ab and Lightfoot had the strain of constant watchfulness upon them.

It may be that because of this ever present peril the two grew closer together. It could not well be otherwise with human beings thus bound and isolated and facing and living upon the rest of nature, part of it seeking always their own lives. They became a wonderfully loving couple, as love went in that rude time. Despite the too wearing outlook imposed upon them, because they were in so dangerous a locality, they were very happy. Yet, one day, came a difference and a hurt.

Oak, apparently forgotten by others, was remembered by Ab, though never spoken of. Sometimes the man had tossed upon his bed of leaves and had muttered in his sleep, and the one word he had most often spoken in this troubled dreaming was the name of Oak. Early in their married life Lightfoot, to whom the memory of the dead man, so little had she known him, was a far less haunting thing than to her husband, had suddenly broken a silence, saying "Where is Oak?" There was no answer,

but the look of the man of whom she had
asked the question was such that she was
glad to creep from his sight unharmed. Yet
once again, months later, she forgot herself
and mocked Ab when he had been boastful
over some exploit of strength and courage and
when he had seemed to say that he knew no
fear. She, but to tease him, sprang up with
a face convulsed and agonized, and with staring eyes and hands opening and shutting, had
cried out "Oak! Oak!" as she had seen Ab do
at night. Her mimic terror was changed on
the moment into reality. With a shudder and
then with a glare in his eyes the man leaped
toward her, snatching his great ax from his
belt and swinging it above her head. The
woman shrieked and shrank to the ground.
The man whirled the weapon aloft and then,
his face twitching convulsively, checked its
descent. He may, in that moment, have
thought of what followed the slaying of the
other who had been close to him. There was
no death done, but, thenceforth, Lightfoot
never uttered aloud the name of Oak. She
became more sedate and grave of bearing.

The episode was but a passing, though not
a forgotten one in the lives of the two. The

months went by and there were tranquil hours in the cave as, at night, the weapons were shaped, and Lightfoot boasted of the arrow-heads she had learned to make so well. Some-times Old Mok would be rowed up the river to them by the sturdy and venturesome Bark, who had grown into a particularly fine youth and who now cared for nothing more than his big brother's admiration. Between Old Mok and Lightfoot, to Ab's great delight, grew up the warmest friendship. The old man taught the woman more of the details of good arrow-making and all he knew of woodcraft in all ways, and the lord of the place soon found his wife giving opinions with an air of the utmost knowledge and authority. Whatever came to him from her and Old Mok pleased him, and when she told him of some of the finer points of arrow-making he stretched out his brawny arms and laughed.

But there came, in time, a shade upon the face of the man. The incident of the talk of Oak may have brought to his mind again more freshly and keenly the memory of the Fire Country. There he had found safety and great comfort. Why should not he and Lightfoot seize upon this home and live there? It was a wonderful place and warm, and there were forests at hand. He became so absorbed in his own thoughts on this great theme that the woman who was his could not understand his mood, but, one day, he told her of what he had been thinking and of what he had resolved upon. "I am going to the Fire Country," he said.

Armed, this time with spear and ax and bow and arrow, and with food abundant in the pouch of his skin garb, Ab left the cave in which Lightfoot was now to stay most of the time, well barricaded, for that she was to hunt afar alone in such a region was not even to be thought of. What thoughts came to the man as he traversed again the forest paths where he had so pondered as he once ran before can be but guessed at. Certainly he had learned no more of Oak.

Lightfoot, left alone in the cave, became at once a most discreet and careful personage, for one of her buoyant and daring temperament. She had often taken risks since her marriage, but there was always the chance of finding within the sound of her voice her big mate, Ab, should danger overtake her. She remained close to the cave, and when early dusk came she lugged the stone barriers into place and built a night-fire within the entrance. The fierce and hungry beasts of the wood came, as usual, lurking and sniffing harshly about the entrance, and when she ventured there and peered outside she saw the wicked and leering eyes. Alone and a little alarmed, she became more vengeful than she would have been with the big, careless Ab beside her. She would have sport with her bow. The advantage of the bow is that it requires no swing of space for its work as is demanded of the flung spear. An arrow may be sent through a mere loophole with no probable demerit as to what it will accomplish. So the woman brought her strongest bow—and far beyond the rough bow of Ab's first make was the bow they now possessed—and gathered together many of the arrows she could make so well and use so well, and, thus equipped, went again to the cave's entrance, and through the space between the heaped rocks of the doorway sent toward the eyes of wolf, or cave hyena, shafts to which they were unaccustomed, but which, somehow, pierced and could find mid-body quite as well as the cave man's spear. There was a certain comfort in the work, though it could not affect her condition in one way or another. It was only something of a gain to drive the eyes away.

And Ab reached the Fire Valley again. He found it as comfortable and untenanted as when the leap through the ring of flame had saved his life. He clambered up the creek and wandered along its banks, where the grass was green because of the warmth about, and studied all the qualities of the naturally defended valley. "I will make my home here," he said. "Lightfoot shall come with me."

The man returned to his cave and his lonely mate again and told her of the Fire Country. He said that in the Fire Valley they would be safer and happier, and told her how he had found an opening underneath the cliff which they could soon enlarge into a cave to meet all wants. Not that a cave was really needed in a fire valley, but they might have one if they cared. And Lightfoot was glad of the departure.

The pair gathered their belongings together and there was the long journey over again which Ab had just accomplished. But it was far different from either journey that he had made. There with him was his wife, and he was all equipped and was to begin a new sort of life which would, he felt, be good. Lightfoot, bearing her load gallantly, was not less jubilant. As a matter of plain fact, though Lightfoot had been happy in the cave in the forest, she had always recognized certain of its disadvantages, as had, in the end, her fearless husband. It is, in a general way, vexatious to live in a locality where, as soon as you leave your hearthstone, you incur, at least, a chance of an exciting and uncomfortable episode and then lodgment in the maw of some imposing creature of the carnivora. Lightfoot was quite ready to seek with Ab the Fire Valley of which he had so often told her. She was a plucky young matron, but there were extremes.

There were no adventures on the journey worth relating. The Fire Valley was reached at nightfall and the two struggled weariedly up the rugged path beside the creek which issued from the valley's western end. As they reached the level Ab threw down his burden, as did Lightfoot, and as the woman's eyes roved over the bright scene, she gave a great gasp of delight. "It is our home!" she cried.

They ate and slept in the light and warmth of surrounding flames, and when the day came they began the work of enlarging what was to be their cave. But, though they worked earnestly, they did not care so much for the prospective shelter as they might have done. What a cave had given was warmth and safety. Here they had both, out of doors and under the clear sky. It was a new and glorious life. Sometimes, though happy, the woman worked a little wearily, and, not long after the settlement of the two in their new home, a child was born to them, a son, robust and sturdy, who came afterward to be known as Little Mok.

CHAPTER XXV.

A GREAT STEP FORWARD.

THERE came to Ab and Lightfoot that comfort which comes with laboring for something desired. In all that the two did amid their pleasant surroundings life became a greater thing because its dangers were so lessened and its burdens lightened. But they were not long the sole human beings in the Fire Valley. There was room for many and soon Old Mok took up his permanent abode with them, for he was most contented when with Ab, who seemed so like a son to him. A cave of his own was dug for Mok, where, with his carving and his making of arrows and spearheads, he was happy in his old age. Soon followed a hegira which made, for the first time, a community. The whole family of Ab, One-Ear, Red-Spot and Bark and Beechleaf and the later ones, all came, and another cave was made, and then old Hilltop was persuaded to follow the example and come with Moonface and Branch and Stone Arm, his big sons, and

the group, thus established and naturally protected, feared nothing which might happen.
The effect of daily counsel together soon made
itself distinctly felt, and, under circumstances
so different, many of the old ways were departed from. Half a mile to the south the
creek, which made a bend adown its course,
tumbled into the river and upon the river
were wild fowl in abundance and in its depths
were fish. The forest abounded in game and
there were great nut-bearing trees and the
wild fruits in their season. Wild bees hovered
over the flowers in the open places and there
were hoards of wild honey to be found in the
hollows of deadened trunks or in the high rock
crevices. A great honey-gatherer, by the way,
was Lightfoot, who could climb so well, and
who, furthermore, had her own fancy for sweet
things. It was either Bark or Moonface who
usually accompanied her on her expeditions,
and they brought back great store of this attractive spoil. The years passed and the
community grew, not merely in numbers, but
intelligence. Though always an adviser with
Old Mok, Ab's chief male companion in adventure was the stanch Hilltop, who was a
man worth hunting with. Having two such

men to lead and with a force so strong behind them the valley people were able to cope with the more dangerous animals venturesomely, and soon the number of these was so decreased that even the children might venture a little way beyond the steep barriers which had been raised where the flame circle had its gaps. The opening to the north was closed by a high stone wall and that along the creek defended as effectively, in a different way. They were having good times in the valley.

At first, the home of all was in the caves dug in the soft rock of the ledge, for of those who came to the novel refuge there was, for a season, none who could sleep in the bright light from the never-waning flames. There came a time, though, when, in midsummer, Ab grumbled at the heat within his cave and he and Lightfoot built for themselves an outside refuge, made of a bark-covered ''lean-to'' of long branches propped against the rock. Thus was the first house made. The habitation proved so comfortable that others in the valley imitated it and soon there was a hive of similar huts along the foot of the overhanging precipice. When the short, sharp winter came, all did not seek their caves again, but the huts were made warmer by the addition to their walls of bark and skins, and cave dwelling in the valley was finally abandoned. There was one exception. Old Mok would not leave his warm retreat, and, as long as he lived, his rock burrow was his home.

There came also, as recruits, young men, friends of the young men of the valley, and the band waxed and waned, for nothing could at once change the roving and independent habits of the cave men. But there came children to the mothers, the broad Moonface being especially to the fore in this regard, and a fine group of youngsters played and straggled up and down the creek and fought valiantly together, as cave children should. The heads of families were friendly, though independent. Usually they lived each without any reference to anyone else, but when a great hunt was on, or any emergency called, the band came together and fought, for the time, under Ab's tacitly admitted leadership. And the young men brought wives from the country round.

The area of improvement widened. Around the Fire Village the zone of safety spread. The roar of the great cave tiger was less often heard within miles of the flaming torches of the valley so inhabited. There grew into existence something almost like a system of traffic, for, from distant parts, hitherto unknown, came other cave men, bringing skins, or flints, or tusks for carving, which they were eager to exchange for the new weapon and for instruction in its uses. Ab was the first chieftain, the first to draw about him a clan of followers. The cave men were taking their·first lesson in a slight, half unconfessed obedience, that first essential of community life where there is yet no law, not even the unwritten law of custom.

Running in and out among the children, sometimes pummeled by them, were a score or two of gray, four-footed, bone-awaiting creatures, who, though as yet uncounted in such relation, were destined to furnish a factor in man's advancement. They were wolves and yet no longer wolves. They had learned to cling to man, but were not yet intelligent enough or taught enough to aid him in his hunting. They were the dogs of the future, the four-footed things destined to become the closest friends of men of future ages, the descendants of the four cubs Ab and Oak had taken from the dens so many years before.

It was humanizing for the children, this association of such a number together, though they ran only a little less wildly than those who had heretofore been born in the isolated caves. There came more of an average of intelligence among them, thus associated, though but little more attention was paid them than the cave men had afforded offspring in the past. There had come to Ab after Little Mok two strong sons, Reindeer and Sure-Aim, very much like him in his youth, but of them, until they reached the age of help and hunting, he saw little. Lightfoot regarded them far more closely, for, despite the many duties which had come upon her, there never disappeared the mother's tenderness and watchfulness. And so it was with Moonface, whose brood was so great, and who was like a noisy hen with chickens. So existed the hovering mother instinct with all the women of the valley, though then the mothers fished and hunted and had stirring events to distract them from domesticity and close affection almost as much as had the men.

From this oddly formed community came a difference in certain ways of doing certain things, which changed man's status, which made a revolution second only to that made

by the bow and for which even men of thought
have not accounted as they should have done,
with the illustration before them in our own
times of what has followed so swiftly the use
of steam and, later, of electricity. Men write
of and wonder at the strange gap between
what are called the Paleolithic and the Neolithic ages, that is, between the ages when the
spearheads and ax and arrowheads were of
stone chipped roughly into shape, and the age
of stone even-edged and smoothly polished.
There was really no gap worth speaking of.
The Paleolithic age changed as suddenly into
the Neolithic as the age of horse power changed
into that of steam and electricity, allowance
being always made for the slower transmission
of a new intelligence in the days when men
lived alone and when a hundred years in the
diffusion of knowledge was as a year to-day.

One day Ab went into Old Mok's cave
grumbling. "I shot an arrow into a great
deer," he said, "and I was close and shot it
with all my force, but the beast ran before it
fell and we had far to carry the meat. I tore
the arrow from him and the blood upon the
shaft showed that it had not gone half way in.
I looked at the arrow and there was a jagged

point uprising from its side. How can a man drive deeply an arrow which is so rough? Are you getting too old to make good spears and arrows, Mok?" And the man fumed a little.

Old Mok made no reply, but he thought long and deeply after Ab had left the cave. Certainly Ab must have good arrows! Was there any way of bettering them? And, the next day, the crippled old man might have been seen looking for something beside the creek where it found its exit from the valley. There were stones ground into smoothness tossed up along the shore and the old man studied them most carefully. Many times he had bent over a stream, watching, thinking, but this time he acted. He noted a small sandstone block against which were rasping stones of harder texture, and he picked this from the tumbling current and carried it to his cave. Then, pouring a little water upon a depression in the stone's face, he selected his best big arrow-head and began rubbing it upon the wet sand-stone. It was a weary work, for flint and sandstone are different things and flint is much the harder, but there came a slow result. Smoother and smoother became the chipped arrowhead, and two days later—for all the waking hours of two days were required in the weary grinding—Old Mok gave to Ab an arrow as smooth of surface and keen of edge as ever flew from bow while stone was used. And not many years passed—as years are counted in old history—before the smoothed stone weaponhead became the common property of cave men. The time of chipped stone had ended and that of smoothed stone had begun. There was no space between them to be counted now. One swiftly became the other. It was a matter of necessity, this exhibition of enterprise and sense by the early man in the prompt general utilization of a new discovery.

And not alone in the improvements in means which came when men of the hunting type were so gathered in a community were the bow and the smoothed implements, though these were the greatest of the discoveries of the epoch. The fishermen who went to the river were not content with the raft-like devices of the aquatic Shell People and learned, in time, that hollowed logs would float and that, with the aid of fire and flint axes, a great log could be hollowed. And never a Phœnician ship-builder, never a Fulton of the steamer, never a modern designer of great yachts, stood higher in the estimation of his fellows than stood the expert in the making of the rude boats, as uncouth in appearance as the river-horse which sometimes upset them, but from which men could, at least, let down their lines or dart their spears to secure the fish in the teeming waters.   And the fishermen had better spears and hooks now, for comparison was necessarily always made among devices, and bone barbs and hooks were whittled out from which the fish no longer often floundered.   There came, in time, the making of rude nets, plaited simply from the tough marsh grasses, but they served the purpose and lessened somewhat the gravity of the great food question.

CHAPTER XXVI.

FACING THE RAIDER.

ONE day, at noon, a man burst, panting, through the wide open entrance to the Fire Valley. His coat of skin was rent and hung awry and, as all could see when he staggered down the pathway, the flesh was torn from one cheek and arm, and down his leg on one side was the stain of dried blood. He was exhausted from his hurt and his run and his talk was, at first, almost unmeaning. He was met by some of the older and wiser among those who saw him coming and to their questions answered only by demanding Ab, who came at once. The hard-breathing and wounded man could only utter the words "Big tiger," when he pitched forward and became unconscious. But his words had been enough. Well understood was it by all who listened what a raid of the cave tiger meant, and there was a running to the gateway and soon was raised the wall of ready stone, upbuilt so high that even the leaping monster

could not hope to reach its summit.   Later
the story of the wounded, but now conscious
and refreshed runner, was told with more of
detail and coherence.

The messenger brought out what he had to
tell gaspingly.   He had lost much blood and
was faint, but he told how there had taken
place something awful in the village of the
Shell Men.   It was but little after dusk the
night before when the Shell Men were gathered
together in merrymaking after good fishing
and lucky gathering of what there was to eat
along the shores of the shell fish and the egg-
laying turtles and the capture of a huge river-
horse.   It had been, up to midnight, one of
the greatest and most joyous meetings the
Shell People had joined in for many years.
They were close-gathered and prosperous and
content, and though there was daily turmoil
and risk of death upon the water and sometimes as great risk upon the land, yet the village fringing the waters had grown, and the
midden—the "kitchen-midden" of future ages
—had raised itself steadily and now stretched
far up and down the creek which was a
river branch and far backward from the creek
toward the forest which ended with the up-

lands. They had learned to dread the forest little, the water people, but from the forest now came what made for each in all the village a dread and horror. The cave tiger had been among them!

The Shell People had gathered together upon the sward fronting their line of shallow caves and one of them, the story-teller and singer, was chanting aloud of the river-horse and the great spoil which was theirs, when there was a hungry roar and the yell or shriek of all, men or women not too stricken by fear to be unable to utter sound, and then the leap into their midst of the cave tiger! Perhaps the story-teller's chant had called the monster's attention to him, perhaps his attitude attracted it; whatever may have been the influence, the tiger seized the singer and leaped lightly into the open beyond the caves and, as lightly, with long bounds, into the blackness of the forest beyond.

There was a moment of awe and horror and then the spirit of the brave Shell Men asserted itself. There was grasping of weapons and an outpouring in pursuit of the devourer. Easy to follow was the trail, for a monster beast carrying a man cannot drop lightly in his leaps.

There was a brief mile or two traversed, though hours were consumed in the search, and then, as morn was breaking, the seekers came upon what was left of the singer. It was not much and it lay across the forest pathway, for the cave tiger did not deign to hide his prey. There came a half moaning growl from the forest. That growl meant lurking death. Then the seekers fled. There was consultation and a resolve to ask for help. So the runner, the man stricken down by a casual stroke in the tiger's rush, but bravest among his tribe, had come to the Fire Valley.

To the panting stranger Ab had not much to say. He saw to it that the man was refreshed and cared for and that the deep scars along his side were dressed after the cave man's fashion. But through the night which followed the great cave leader pondered deeply. Why should men thus live and dread the cave tiger? Surely men were wiser than any beast! This one monster must, anyhow, be slain!

But little it mattered to all surrounding nature that the strong man in the Fire Valley had resolved upon the death of the cave tiger. The tiger was yet alive! There was a difference in the pulse of all the woodland. There was a hush throughout the forest. The word, somehow, went to every nerve of all the world of beasts, ''Sabre-Tooth is here!'' Even the huge cave bear shuffled aside as there came to him the scent of the invader. The aurochs and the urus, the towering elk, the reindeer and the lesser horned and antlered things fled wildly as the tainted air brought to them the tale of impending murder. Only the huge rhinoceros and mammoth stood their ground, and even these were terror-stricken with regard for their guarded young whenever the tiger neared them. The rhinoceros stood then, fierce-fronted and dangerous, its offspring hovering by its flanks, and the mammoths gathered in a ring encircling their calves and presenting an outward range of tusks to meet the hovering devourer. The dread was all about. The forest became seemingly nearly lifeless. There was less barking and yelping, less reckless playfulness of wild creatures, less rustling of the leaves and pattering along the forest paths. There was fear and quiet, for Sabre-Tooth had come!

The runner, refreshed and strengthened by food and sleep, appeared before Ab in the morning and told his story more in detail and got in return the short answer: "We will go with you and help you and your people. Tigers must be killed!"

Rarely before had man gone out voluntarily to hunt the great cave tiger. He had, sometimes in awful strait, defended himself against the monster as best he could, but to seek the encounter where the odds were so great against him was an ugly task. Now the man-slayer was to be the pursued instead of the pursuer. It required courage. The vengeful wounded man looked upon Ab with a grim, admiring regard. "You fear not?" he said.

There was bustling in the valley and soon a stalwart dozen men were armed with bow and spear and the journey was taken up toward the Shell Men's home. The village was reached at mid-day and as the little troop emerged from the forest the death wail fell upon their ears. "The tiger has come again!" exclaimed the runner.

It was true. The tiger had come again! Once more with his stunning roar he had swept through the village and had taken another victim, a woman, the wife of one of the head men. Too benumbed by fear, this time, to act at once, the Shell Men had not pursued the great brute into the darkness. They had but ventured out in the morning and followed the trail and found that the tiger had carried the woman in very nearly the same direction as he had borne the man and that what remained from his gorging of the night lay where his earlier feast had been. It was the first tragedy almost repeated.

The little group of Fire Valley folk entered the village and were received with shouts from the men, while from the throats of the women still rose the death wail. There were more people about the huts than Ab had ever seen there and he recognized at once among the group many of the cave men from the East, strong people of his own kind. As the wounded runner had gone to the Fire Valley, so another had been sent to the East, to call upon another group for aid, and the Eastern cave people, under the leadership of a huge, swarthy man called Boarface, had come to learn what the strait was and to decide upon what degree of help they could afford to give. Between these Eastern and the Western cave men there was a certain coldness. There was no open enmity, though at some time in the past there had been family battles and memories of feuds were still existent.   But Ab and Boarface met genially and there was not a trace of difference now.   Boarface joined readily in the council which was held and decided that he would aid in the desperate hunt, and certainly his aid was not to be despised when his followers were looked upon.   They were a stalwart lot.

The way was taken by the gathered fighting men toward where, across the forest path, lay part of a woman.   As the place was neared the band gathered close together and there were outpointing spears, just as the mammoths' tusks outpointed when the beasts guarded their young from the thing now hunted.   But there came no attack and no sound from the forest.   The tiger must be sleeping.   Beneath a huge tree bordering the pathway lay what remained of the woman's body.   Fifty feet above, and almost directly over this dreadful remnant of humanity, shot out a branch as thick as a man's body.   There was consultation among the hunters and in this Ab took the lead, while Boarface and the Shell Men who had come to help assented readily.   No need existed for the risk of an open fight with this great beast.   Craft must be used and Ab gave forth his swift commands.

The Fire Valley leader had seen to it that his company had brought what he needed in his effort to kill the tiger. There were two great tanned, tough urus hides. There were lengths of rhinoceros hide, cut thickly, which would endure a strain of more than the weight of ten brawny men. There was one spear, with a shaft of ashwood at least fifteen feet in length and as thick as a man's wrist. Its head was a blade of hardest flint, but the spear was too heavy for a man's hurling. It had been made for another use.

There was little hesitation in what was done, for Ab knew well the quality of the work he had in hand. He unfolded his plan briefly and then he himself climbed to the tree-top and out upon the limb, carrying with him the knotted strip of rhinoceros hide. In the pouch of his skin garment were pebbles. He reached a place on the big limb overhanging the path and dropped a pebble. It struck the earth a yard or two away from what remained of the woman's body and he shouted to those below to drag the mangled body to the spot where the pebble had hit the earth. They were about to do so when from the forest on one side of the path came a roar, so

appalling in every way that there was no
thought of anything among most of the workers save of sudden flight. The tiger was in
the wood and very near and a scent had
reached him. There was a flight which left
upon the ground beneath the tree branches
only old Hilltop and the rough Boarface and
some dozen sturdy followers, these about
equally divided between the East and the
West men of the hills. There was swift and
sharp work then.

The tiger might come at any moment, and
that meant death to one at least. But those
who remained were brave men and they had
come far to encompass this tiger's ending.
They dragged what remained of the tiger's
prey to where the pebble had hit the earth.
Ab, clinging and raging aloft, afar out upon
the limb, shouted to Hilltop to bring him the
spear and the urus skins, and soon the sturdy
old man was beside him. Then, about two
deep notches in the huge shaft, thongs were
soon tied strongly, and just below its middle
were attached the bag-shaped urus skins.
Near its end the rhinoceros thong was knotted
and then it was left hanging from the limb
supported by this strong rope, while, three-

fourths of the way down its length, dangled
on each side the two empty bags of hide.
Short orders were given, and, directed by
Boarface, one man after another climbed the
tree, each with a weight of stones carried in
his pouch, and each delivering his load to old
Hilltop, who, lying well out upon the limb,
passed the stones to Ab, who placed them in
the skin pouches on either side the suspended
and threatening spear. The big skin pouches
on either side were filling rapidly, when there
came from the forest another roar, nearer and
more appalling than before, and some of the
workers below fled panic-stricken. Ab shouted
and frothed and foamed as the men ran. Old
Hilltop slid down the tree, ax in hand, followed
by the dark Boarface, and one or two of the
men below were captured and made to work
again. Soon all the work which Ab had in
mind was done. Above the path, just over
what remained of the woman, hung the great
spear, weighted with half a thousand pounds
of stone and sure to reach its mark should the
tiger seek its prey again. The branch was
broad and the line of rhinoceros skin taut, and
Ab's flint knife was keen of edge. Only courage and calmness were needed in the dread

presence of the monster of the time. Neither
the swarthy Boarface nor the gaunt Hilltop
wanted to leave him, but Ab forced them
away.

Not long to wait had the cave man, but the
men who had been with him were already
distant. The shadows were growing long now,
but the light was still from the sunshine of the
early afternoon. The man lying along the
limb, knife in hand, could hear no sound save
the soft swish of leaves against each other as
the breeze of later day pushed its way through
the forest, or the alarmed cries of knowing
birds who saw on the ground beneath them a
huge thing slip along with scarce a sound from
the impact of his fearfully clawed but padded
feet as he sought the meal he had prepared
for himself. The great beast was approaching. The great man aloft was waiting.

Into the open along the path came the tiger,
and Ab, gripping the limb more firmly, looked
down upon the thing so closely and in daylight
for the first time in his life. Ab was certainly
brave, and he was calm and wise and thinking
beyond his time, but when he saw plainly this
beast which had slipped so easily and silently
from the forest, safe though he was upon his

perch, he was more than startled. The thing was so huge and with an aspect so terrible to look upon!

The great cat's head moved slowly from side to side; the baleful eyes blazed up and down the pathway and the tawny muzzle was lifted to catch what burden there might be on the air. The beast seemed satisfied, emerging fairly into the sunlight. Immense of size but with the graceful lankness of the tigers of to-day, Sabre-Tooth somewhat resembled them, though, beside him, the largest inmate of the Indian jungle would appear but puny. The creature Ab looked upon that day so long ago was beautiful, in his way. He was beautiful as is the peacock or the banded rattle-snake. There were color contrasts and fine blendings. The stripes upon him were wonderfully rich, and as he came creeping toward the body, he was as splendid as he was dreadful.

With every nerve strained, but with his first impulse of something like terror gone, Ab watched the devourer beneath him while his sharp flint knife, hard gripped, bore lightly against the taut rhinoceros-hide rope. The tiger began his ghastly meal but was not quite beneath the suspended spear. Then came

some distant sound in the forest and he raised
his head and shifted his position. He was
fairly under the spear now. The knife pressed
firmly against the rawhide was drawn back
and forth noiselessly but with effectiveness.
Suddenly the last tissue parted and the enor-
mously-weighted spear fell like a lightning-
stroke. The broad flint head struck the tiger
fairly between the shoulders, and, impelled by
such a weight, passed through his huge body
as if it had met no obstacle. Upon the strong
shaft of ash the monster was impaled. There
echoed and reëchoed through the forest a roar
so fearful that even the hunters whom Ab had
sent far away from the scene of the tragedy
clambered to the trees for refuge. The struggles of the pierced brute were tremendous beyond description, but no strength could avail
it now; it had received its death wound and
soon the great tiger lay still, as harmless as
the squirrel, frightened and hidden in his nest.
In wild triumph Ab slid to the ground and
then the long cry to summon his party went
echoing through the wood. When the others
found him he had withdrawn the spear and
was already engaged, flint knife in hand, in

stripping from the huge body the glorious robe it wore.

There was excitement and rejoicing. The terror had been slain! The Shell People were frantic in their exultation. Meanwhile Ab had called upon his own people to assist him and the wonderful skin of the tiger was soon stretched out upon the ground, a glorious possession for a cave man.

"I will have half of it," declared Boarface, and he and Ab faced each other menacingly. "It shall not be cut," was the fierce retort. "It is mine. I killed the tiger!"

Strong hands gripped stone axes and there was chance of deadly fray then and there, but the Shell People interfered and the Shell People excelled in number, and were a potent influence for peace. Ab carried away the splendid trophy, but as Boarface and his men departed, there were black faces and threatening words.

CHAPTER XXVII.

LITTLE MOK.

AMONG all the children of Ab—and remarkable it was for the age—the best loved was Little Mok, the eldest son. When the child, strong and joyous, was scarcely two years old, he fell from a ledge off the cliff where he had climbed to play, and both his legs were broken. Strange to say he survived the accident in that time when the law of the survival of the fittest was almost invariable in its sternest and most purely physical demonstration. The mother love of Lightfoot warded off the last pitiless blow of nature, although the child, a hopeless cripple, never after walked. The name Little Mok was naturally given him, and before long the child had won the heart, as well as the name, of the limping old maker of axes, spearheads and arrows.

The closer ties of family life, as we know them now, existed but in their outlines to the cave man. The man and woman were faithful to each other with the fidelity of the higher animals and their children were cared for with rough tenderness in their infancy. The time of absolute dependence was made very short, though, and children very early were required to find some of their own food, and taught by necessity to protect themselves. But Little Mok, unable to take up for himself the burden of an independent existence, was not slain nor left to die of neglect as might have been another child thus crippled in the time in which he lived. He, once spared, grew into the wild hearts of those closest to him and became the guarded and cherished one of the rude home of Ab and Lightfoot, and to him was thus given the continuous love and care which the strong-limbed boys and girls of the family lost and never missed.

It was a strange thing for the time. The child had qualities other than the negative ones of helplessness and weakness with which to bind to him the hearts of those around him, but the primary fact of his entire dependence upon them was what made him the center of the little circle of untaught, untamed cave people who lived in the Fire Valley. He may have been the first child ever so cherished from such impulse.

From his mother the child inherited a joyous disposition which nothing could subdue. Often on the return home from some little expedition on which it had been practicable to take him, sitting on Lightfoot's shoulder, or on the still stronger arm of old One-Ear, his silent, somewhat brooding grandfather, the little brown boy made the woods ring with shrill bird calls, or the mimicry of animals, and ever his laughter filled the spaces in between these sounds. Other children flocked around the merry youngster, seeking to emulate his play of voice and the oldsters smiled as they saw and heard the joyous confusion about the tiny reveler. The excursions to the river were Little Mok's chief delight from his early childhood. He entered into the preparations for them with a zest and keen enjoyment born of the presence of an adventurous spirit in a maimed body, and when the fishing party left the Fire Camp it was incomplete if Little Mok was not carried lightly at the van, the life and joy of the occasion.

No one ever forgot the day when Little Mok, then about six years old, caught his first fish. His joy and pride infected all as he exhibited his prize and boasted of what he would catch in the river next, and when, on the return, Old Mok saluted him as the "Great Fisherman," the elf's elation became too great for any expression. His little chest heaved, his eyes flashed, and then he wriggled from Lightfoot's arms into the lap of Old Mok, snuggled down into the old man's furs and hid his face there; and the two understood each other.

It was soon after this great event of the first fish-catching that Red-Spot, Ab's mother, died. She had never quite adapted herself to the new life in the Fire Valley, and after a time she began to grow old very fast. At last a fever attacked her and the end of her patient, busy life came. After her death One-Ear was much in Old Mok's cave, the two had so long been friends. There with them the crippled boy was often to be found. He was not always gay and joyous. Sometimes he lay for days on his bed of leaves at home, in weakness and pain, silent and unlike himself. Then when Lightfoot's care had given him back a little strength, he would beg to be taken to Old Mok's cave. There he could sleep, he said, away from the noise and the lights of the outside world, and finally he claimed and was allowed a nest of his own in the warmest and

darkest nook of Old Mok's den, where he slept
every night, and sometimes a good part of the
day, when one of his times of pain and weakness was upon him.   Here during many a long
hour of work, experiment and argument, the
wide eyes and quick ears of Little Mok saw and
heard, while Ab, Mok and One-Ear bent over
their work at arrowhead or spear point, and
talked of what might be done to improve the
weapons upon which so much depended. Here,
when no one else remained in the weary darkness of night and the half light of stormy days
Old Mok beguiled the time with stories, and
sometimes in a hoarse voice even attempted to
chant to his little hearer snatches of the wild
singing tales of the Shell People, for the Shell
People had a sort of story song.

Once, when Lightfoot sat by Old Mok's
fire, she told them of the time when she and
Ab found themselves outside their cave,
unarmed, with a bear to be eaten through
before they could get into their door, and
Little Mok surprised his mother and Old Mok
by an outburst of laughter at the tale. He
had a glimmering of humor, and saw the
droll side of the adventure, a view which had
not occurred to Lightfoot, nor to Ab.   The

little lad, of the world, yet not in it, saw
vaguely the surprises, lights and shades and
contrasts of existence, and sometimes they
made him laugh. The laugh of the cave
man was not a common event, and when it
came was likely to be sober and sardonic, at
least it was so when not simply an evidence
of rude health and high animal spirits. Humor is one of the latest, as it is one of the
most precious, grains shaken out of Time's
hour-glass, but Little Mok somehow caught
a tiny bit of the rainbow gift, long before its
time in the world, and soon, with him, it
was to disappear for centuries to come.

One day when Little Mok was brought back
from an expedition to the river, he told Old
Mok how he had sat long on the bank, too
tired to fish, and had just rested and feasted
his eyes on the wood, the stream, the small
darting creatures in it, the birds, and the
animals which came to drink. Describing a
herd of reindeer which had passed near him,
Little Mok took up a piece of Old Mok's red
chalkstone and on the wall of the cave drew
a picture of the animal. The veteran stared
in surprise. The picture was wonderfully
life-like in grasp and detail. The child owned

that great gift, the memory of sight, and his hand was cunning. Encouraged by his success, the boy drew on, delighting Old Mok with his singular fidelity and skill. Then came hours and days of sketching and etching in the old man's cave. The master was delighted. He brought out from their hiding places his choicest pieces of mammoth tusk or teeth of the river-horse for Little Mok's etchings and carvings. And, as time passed, the young artist excelled the old one, and became the pride and boast of his friend and teacher. Sometimes the little lad would work far into the night, for he could not pause when he had begun a thing until it was complete—but then he would sleep in his warm nest until noon the next day, crawling out to cook a bit of meat for himself at the nearest fire, or sharing Old Mok's meal, as was more convenient.

While everything else in the Fire Valley was growing, developing and flourishing, Little Mok's frail body had ever grown but slowly, and about the beginning of his twelfth year there appeared a change in him. He became permanently weak and grew more and more helpless day by day. His cherished excursions to the river, even his little journeys on old One-Ear's strong arm to the cliff top, from whence he could see the whole world at once, had all to be abandoned.

When the winter snows began to whirl in the air Little Mok was lying quietly on his bed, his great eyes looking wistfully up at Lightfoot, who in vain taxed her limited skill and resources to tempt him to eat and become more sturdy. She hovered over him like a distressed mother bird over its youngling fallen from the nest, but, with all her efforts, she could not bring back even his usual slight measure of health and strength to the poor Little Mok. Ab came sometimes and looked sadly at the two and then walked moodily away, a great weight on his breast. Old Mok was always at work, and yet always ready to give Little Mok water or turn his weary little frame on its rude bed, or spread the furs over the wasted body, and always Lightfoot waited and hoped and feared.

And at last Little Mok died, and was buried under the stones, and the snow fell over the lonely cairn under the fir trees outside the Fire Valley where his grave was made.

Lightfoot was silent and sad, and could not

smile nor laugh any more. She longed for
Little Mok, and did not eat or sleep. One
night Ab, trying to comfort her, said, ''You
will see him again.''

''What do you mean?'' cried Lightfoot.
And Ab only answered, ''You will see him; he
will come at night. Go to sleep, and you
will see him.''

But Lightfoot could not sleep yet and for
many a night her eyes closed only when ex-
treme fatigue compelled sleep toward the
morning.

And at last, after many days and nights,
Lightfoot, when asleep, saw Little Mok.
Just as in life, she saw him, with all his familiar looks and motions. But he did not stay
long. And again and again she saw him, and
it comforted her somewhat because he smiled.
There had come to her such a heartache
about him, lying out there under the snow
and stones, with no one to care for him, that
the smile warmed her heavy heart and she
told Ab that she had seen Little Mok, only
whispering it to him—for it was not well, she
knew, to talk about such things—and she
whispered to Ab, too, her anguish that Little
Mok only came at night, and never when it

was day, but she did not complain.   She only said: "I want to see him in the daytime."

And Ab could think of nothing to say. But that made him think more and more.   He felt drawn closer to Lightfoot, his wife, no longer a young girl, but the mother of Little Mok, who was dead, and of all his children.

In his mind arose, vaguely obscure, yet persistent, the idea that brute strength and vigor, keen senses and reckless bravery were not, after all, the sole qualities that make and influence men.   Old Mok, crippled and disabled for the hunt and defense, was nevertheless a power not to be despised, and Little Mok, the helpless child, had been still strong enough to win and keep the love of all the stalwart and rough cave people.   Ab was sorry for Lightfoot.   When in the spring the forlorn mother held in her arms a baby girl a little brightness came into her eyes again, and Ab, seeing this, was glad, but neither Ab nor Lightfoot ever forgot their eldest and dearest, Little Mok.

CHAPTER XXVIII.

THE BATTLE OF THE BARRIERS.

WHILE Ab had been occupied by home affairs
trouble for him and his people had been brew-
ing.   By no means unknown to each other
before the tiger hunt were Ab and Boarface.   They had hunted together and once
Boarface, with half a dozen companions, had
visited the Fire Valley and had noted its many
attractions and advantages.   Now Boarface
had gone away angry and muttering, and he
was not a man to be thought of lightly.   His
rage over the memory of Ab's trophy did not
decrease with the return to his own region.
Why should this cave man of the West have
sole possession of that valley, which was warm
and green throughout the winter and where
the wild beasts could not enter?   Why had
he, this Ab, been allowed to go away with all
the tiger's skin?   Brooding enlarged into resolve and Boarface gathered together his relations and adherents.   "Let us go and take the
Fire Valley of Ab," he said to them, and,

gradually, though objections were made to the undertaking of an enterprise so fraught with danger, the listeners were persuaded.

"There are other fires far down the river," said one old man. "Let us go there, if it is fire we most need, and so we will not disturb nor anger Ab, who has lived in his valley for many years. Why battle with Ab and all his people?"

But Boarface laughed aloud: "There are many other earth fires," he said. "I know them well, but there is no other fire which chances to make a flaming fence about a valley close to the great rocks, and which has water within the space it surrounds and which makes a wall against all the wild beasts. We will fight and win the valley of Ab."

And so they were led into the venture. They sought, too, the aid of the Shell People in this raid, but were not successful. The Shell People were not unfriendly to those of the Fire Valley, and had not Ab been really the one to kill the tiger? Besides, it was not wise for the waterside dwellers to engage in any controversy between the forest factions, for the hill people had memories and heavy axes. A few of the younger and more adventurous joined the force of Boarface, but the alliance had no tribal sanction.   Still, the force of the swarthy leader of the Eastern cave men was by no means insignificant.   It contained good fighting men, and, when runners had gone far and wide in the Eastern country, there were gathered nearly ten score of hunters who could throw the spear or wield the ax and who were not fearful of their lives.   The band led by Boarface started for the Fire Country, intending to surprise the people in the valley.   They moved swiftly, but not so swiftly as a fleet young man from the Shell People who preceded them.   He was sent by the elders a day before the time fixed for the assault, and so Ab learned all about the intended raid.   Then went forth runners from the valley; then the matron Lightfoot's eyes became fiery, since Ab was threatened; then old Hilltop looked carefully over his spears, and poised thoughtfully his great stone ax; then Moonface smote her children and gathered together certain weapons, and then Old Mok went into his cave and stayed there, working at none knew what.

They came from all about, the Western cave men, for never in the valley had food or shelter been refused to any and the Eastern cave men were not loved. Many a quarrel over game had taken place between the raging hunters of the different tribes, and many a bloody single-handed encounter had come in the depths of the forest. The band was not a large one, the Eastern men being far more numerous, but the outlook was not as fine as it might be for the advancing Boarface. The force assembled inside the valley was, in point of numbers, but little more than half his own, but it was in-trenched and well-armed, and there were those among the defenders whom it was not well to meet in fight. But Boarface was confident and was not dismayed when his force crept into the open only to find the ordinary valley entrance barred and all preparations made for giving him a welcome of the warmer sort. There was what could not be thoroughly bar-ricaded in so brief a time, the entrance where the brook issued at the west. This pass must be forced, for the straight, uprising wall be-tween the flames and across the opening to the north was something relatively unassail-able. It was too narrow and too high and sheer and there were too many holes in the wall through which could be sent those piercing arrows which the Western cave men knew how to use so well.   The battle must be up along the bed of the little creek.   The water was low at this season, so low that a man might wade easily anywhere, and there had been erected only a slight barrier, enough to keep wild beasts away, for Ab had never thought of invasion by human beings.   The creek tumbled downward, through passages, between straight-sided, ruggedly built stone heaps, with spaces between wide enough to admit a man, but not any great beast of prey.   There was no place where, by a man, the wall could not easily be mounted and, above, there was no really good place of vantage for the defenders.

So the invading force, concealment of action being no longer necessary, ranged themselves along the banks of the creek to the west of the valley and prepared for a rush.   They had certain chances in their favor.   They were strong men, who knew how to use their weapons well, and they were in numbers almost as two to one.   Meanwhile, inside the valley, where the approach and plans of the enemy had been seen and understood, there had gone on swiftly, under Ab's stern direction, such preparation for the fray as seemed most adequate with the means at hand.

The great advantage possessed was that the defenders, on firm footing themselves, could meet men climbing, and so, a little further up the creek than the beast-opposing wall, had been thrown up what was little more than a rude platform of rock, wide and with a broad expanse of top, on which all the valley's force might cluster in an emergency. Upon this the people were to gather, defending the first pass, if they could, by flights of spears and arrows and here, at the end, to win or lose. This was the general preparation for the onslaught, but there had been precautions taken more personal and more involving the course of the most important of the people of the valley.

At the left of the gorge, where must come the invaders, the rock rose sheerly and at one place extended outward a shelf, high up, but reached easily from the Fire Valley side. There were consultations between Ab and the angry and anxious and almost tearful Lightfoot. That charming lady, now easily the best archer of the tribe, had developed at once into a fighting creature and now demanded that her place be assigned to her. With her own bow, and with arrows in quantity, it was decided that she should occupy the ledge and do all she could. Upon the ledge was comparative safety in the fray, and Ab directed that she should go there. Old Hilltop said but little. It was understood, almost as a matter of course, that he would be upon the barrier and there face, with Ab, the greatest issue. The old man was by no means unsatisfactory to look upon as he moved silently about and got ready the weapons he might have to use. Gaunt, strong-muscled and resolute, he was worthy of admiration. Ever following him with her eyes, when not engaged in the chastisement of one of her swart brood, was Moonface, for Moonface had long since learned to regard her grizzled lord with love as well as much respect.

There were other good fighting men and other women beside these mentioned who would do their best, but these few were the dominant figures. Meanwhile, Boarface and his strong band had decided upon their plan of attack and would soon rush up the bed of the shallow stream with all the bravery and ferocity of those who were accustomed to face death lightly and to seize that which they wanted.

The invaders came clambering up the creek's course, openly and with menacing and defiant shouts, for any concealment was now out of the question. They had but few bows and could, under the conditions, send no arrow flight which would be of avail, but they had thews and sinews and spears and axes. As they came with such rush as men might make up a tumbling waterway with slipping pebbles beneath the feet and forced themselves one by one between the heaped stone piles and fairly in front of the barrier there was a discharge of arrows and more than one man, impaled by a stone-headed shaft, fell, to dabble feebly in the water, and did not rise again. But there came a time in the fight when the bow must be abandoned.

The assault was good and the demeanor of the men behind the barrier was good as well. Not more gallant was one group than the other for there were splendid fighters in both ranks. The boasted short sword of the Romans, in times effeminate, as compared with these, afforded not in its wielding a greater test of personal courage than the handling of the flint-headed spear or the stone knife or chipped ax. There, all along the barrier, was the real grappling of man and man, with further existence as the issue.

The invaders, losing many of their number, for arrows flew steadily and a mass so large could not easily be missed even by the most bungling of those strong archers, swept upward to the barrier and then was a muscular, deadly tumult worth the seeing. To the south and nearest the side where Lightfoot was perched with her bow and great bunch of arrows Ab stood in front, while to his right and near the other end of the rude stone rampart was stationed old Hilltop, and he hurled his spears and slew men as they came. The fight became simply a death struggle, with the advantage of position upon one side and of numbers on the other. And Ab and Boarface were each seeking the other.

So the struggle lasted for a long half hour, and when it ended there were dead and dying men upon the barrier, while the waters of the creek were reddened by the blood of the slain assailants. The assault now ebbed a little. Neither Ab nor Hilltop had been injured in the struggle. As the invaders pressed close Ab had noted the whish of an arrow now and then and the hurt to one pressing him closely, and old Hilltop had heard the wild cries of a woman who hovered in his rear and hurled stones in the faces of those who strove to reach him. And now there came a lull.

Boarface had recognized the futility of scaling, under such conditions, a steep so well defended and had thought of a better way to gain his end and crush Ab and his people. He had heard the story of Ab's first advent into the valley when, chased by the wolves, he leaped through the flame, and there came an inspiration to him! What one man had done others could do, and, with picked warriors of his band, he made a swift detour, while, at the same time, the main body rushed desperately upon the barrier again.

What had been good fighting before was better now. Lives were lost, and soon all arrows were spent and all spears thrown, and then came but the dull clashing of stone axes. Ab raged up and down, and, ever in the front, faced the oncoming foe and slew as could slay the strong and utterly desperate. More than once his life was but a toy of chance as men sprang toward him, two or three together, but ever at such moment there sang an arrow by his head and one of his assailants, pierced in throat or body, fell back blindly, hampering his companions, whose heads Ab's great ax was seeking fiercely. And, all the time, nearer the northern end of the barrier, old Hilltop fought serenely and dreadfully. There were many dead men in the pools of the creek between the barrier and the entrance to the valley. And about Ab ever sang the arrows from the rocky shelf.

There was wild clamor, the clash of weapons and the shouting of battle-crazed men but there was not enough to drown the sound of a scream which rose piercingly above the din. Ab recognized the voice of Lightfoot and raised his eyes to see the woman, regardless of her own safety, standing upright and pointing up the valley. He knew that something meaning life and death was happening and that he must go. He leaped backward and a huge Western cave man sprang to his place, to serve as best he could.

Not a moment too soon had that shrill cry reached the ears of the fighting man. He ran backward, shouting to a score of his people to follow him as he ran, and in an instant recognized that he had been outwitted, at least for the moment, by the vengeful Boarface. As he rushed to the east toward the wall of flame he saw a dark form pass through its crest in a flying leap. There were others he knew would follow. His own feat of long ago was being repeated by Boarface and his chosen group of best men!

It was not Boarface who leaped and it was hard for a gallant youth of the Eastern cave men that he had strength and daring and had dashed ahead in the assault, for he had scarcely touched the ground when there sank deeply into his head a stone ax, impelled by the strongest arm of all that region, and he was no more among things alive. Ab had reached the fire wall with the speed of a great runner while, close behind him, came his eager following.

The forces could see each other clearly enough now, and those on the outside outnumbered those on the inside again by two to one. But those leaping the flames could not alight poised ready for a blow, and there were adroit and vengeful axmen awaiting them. There was a momentary pause for planning among the assailants, and then it was that Ab fumed over his own lack of foresight. His chosen band who were with him now were all bow-

men, and about the shoulder and chest of each
was still slung his weapon, but there were no
more arrows.   Each quiverful had been shot
away early in the fight and then had come
the spear and ax play.   But what a chance
for arrows now, with that threatening band
preparing for the rush and leap together, and,
while out of reach of spear or ax, within easy
reach of the singing little shafts!   Oh, for the
shafts now, those slender barbed things which
were hurled in his new way!   And, even as
he thus raged, there came a feeble shout from
down the valley behind him and he saw something very good!

Limping, with effort, but resolutely forward,
was a bent old man, bearing encircled within
his long arms a burden which Ab himself could
not have carried for any distance without
stress and labored breathing.   The lean old
Mok's arms were locked about a monster sheaf
of straight flint-headed arrows, a sheaf greater
in size than ever man had looked upon before.
The crippled veteran had not been idle in his
cave.   He had worked upon the store of shafts
and flintheads he had accumulated, and here
was the result in a great emergency!

The old man cast his sheaf upon the ground

and then sank down, somewhat totteringly, beside it.   There needed no shout of command from Ab to tell those about him what to do. There was one combined yell of sudden exultation, a rush together for the shafts and a swift filling of empty quivers.   It was but the work of a moment or two.   Then something promptly happened. The great fellows, though acting without orders, shot almost "all to-gether," as the later English archers did, and so close just across the flame wall was the opposing group that the meanest archer in all the lot could scarcely fail to reach a living target, and stronger arms drew back those arrows than were the arms of those who drew bowstring in the battles of mediæval history. With the first deadly flight came a scattering outside and men lay tossing upon the ground in their death agony.   There was no cessation to the shot, though Boarface sought fiercely to rally his followers, until all had fled beyond the range of the bowmen.   Upon the ground were so many dead that the numbers of the two forces were now more nearly equal.   But Boarface had brave followers.   They ranged themselves together at a safe distance and then started for the flame wall with a rush, to leap it all together.

There was another arrow-flight as the onslaught came, and more men went down, but the charge could not be stopped. Over the low flame-crests shot a great mass of bodies, there to meet that which was not good for them. The struggle was swift and deadly, but the forces were almost evenly matched now and the insiders had the advantage. Boarface and Ab met face to face in the melée and each leaped toward the other with a yell. There was to be a fight which must be excellent, for two strong leaders were meeting and there were many lives at stake.

CHAPTER XXIX.

OLD HILLTOP'S LAST STRUGGLE.

EVEN as he leaped the flames, the desperate Boarface hurled at Ab a fragment of stone, which was a thing to be wisely dodged, and the invader was fairly on his feet and in position to face his adversary as the axes came together. More active, more powerful, it may be, and certainly more intelligent, was Ab than Boarface, but the leader of the assailants had been a raider from early youth and knew how to take advantage. In those fierce days to attain the death of an enemy, in any way, was the practical end sought in a conflict. Close behind Boarface had leaped a youth to whom the leader had given his commands before the onrush and who, as he found his feet upon the valley's sward, sought, not an adversary face to face, but circled about the two champions, seeking only to get behind the leaping Ab while Boarface occupied his sole attention. The young man bore a great stone-headed club, a dreadful weapon in such hands

as his. The men struck furiously and flakes
spun from the heavy axes, but Boarface was
being slowly driven back when there descended
upon Ab's shoulder a blow which swerved him
and would certainly have felled a man with
less heaped brawn to meet the impact. At
the same instant Boarface made a fierce
downward stroke and Ab leaped aside without
parrying or returning it, for his arm was
numbed. Another such blow from the new
assailant and his life was lost, yet he dare not
turn. That would be his death. And now
Boarface rushed in again and as the axes came
together called to his henchman to strike more
surely.

And just then, just as it seemed to Ab the
end was near, he heard behind him the sharp
twang of the bowstring which had sounded so
sweetly at the valley's other end and, with a
groan, there pitched down upon the sward
beside him a writhing man whose legs drew
back and forth in agony and who had been
pierced by an arrow shot fiercely and closely
from behind and driven in between his shoulder
blades. He knew what it must mean. The
arm which had drawn that arrow to its head
was that of a slight, strong creature who was

not a man.   Lightfoot, wild with love and anxiety, had shot past Old Mok just as he laid down his bundle of arrows, and, when she saw her husband's peril, had leaped forward with arrow upon string and slain his latest assailant in the nick of time.   Now, with arrow notched again and a face ablaze with murderous helpfulness, she hovered near, intent only upon sending a second shaft into the breast of Boarface.

But there was no need.   Unhampered now, Ab rushed in upon his enemy and rained such blows as only a giant could have parried. Boarface fought desperately, but it was only man to man, and he was not the equal of the maddened one before him.   His ax flew from his hand as his wrist was broken by Ab's descending weapon, and the next moment he fell limply and hardly moved, for a second blow had sunk the stone weapon so deeply in his head that the haft was hidden in his long hair.

It was all over in a moment now.   As Ab turned with a shout of triumph there was a swift end to the little battle.   There were brief encounters here and there, but the Eastern men were leaderless and less well-equipped than their foes, and though they fought as desperately as cornered wolves, there was no hope for them. Three escaped. They fled wildly toward the flame and leaped over and through its flickering yellow crest and there was no pursuit. It was not a time for besieged men to be seeking useless vengeance. There came wild yells from the lower end of the valley where the greater fight was on. With a cry Ab gathered his men together and the victorious band ran toward the barrier again, there with overwhelming force to end the struggle. Ever, in later years, did Ab regret that his fight with Boarface had not ended sooner. To save an old hero he had come too late.

Boarface, when taking with him a strong band to the upper end of the valley, had still left a supposably overwhelming force to fight its way up and over the barrier. Ab away from the scene of struggle, old Hilltop assumed command. He was a fit man for such death-facing steadfastness as was here required.

Never had Ab been able to persuade Light-foot's father to use or even try the new weapon, the bow and arrow. He had no tender feeling toward modern innovations. He had a clear eye and strong arm, and the ax and spear

were good enough for him! He recognized
Ab's great qualities, but there were some things
that even a well-regarded son-in-law could not
impose upon any elder family male. Among
these was this twanging bow with its light shaft,
better fitted for a child's plaything than for
real work among men. As for him, give him
a heavy spear, with the blade well set in thongs,
or a heavy ax, with the head well clinched in
the sinew-bound wooden haft. There was
rarely miss or failure to the spear-thrust or the
ax-stroke. And now, in proof of the sound-
ness of his old-fashioned belief, he staked ruggedly his life. There were few spears left.
There were only axes on either side. And
there stood old Hilltop upon the barrier, while
beside him and all across stood men as brave
if not quite as sturdy or as famous.

In the rear of the line, noisy, sometimes
fierce and sometimes weeping, were the women,
whose skill was only a little less than that of
the males and who were even more ruthless in
all feeling toward the enemy. And still easily
chief among these, conspicuous by her noisy
and uncaring demeanor of mingled alarm and
vengefulness, was the raging Moonface. She
rushed up close beside her husband's defend-

ing group and still hurled stones and hurled them most effectively. They went as if from a catapult, and more than one bone or head was broken that day by those missiles from the arm of this squat savage wife and mother. But the men below were outnumbering and brave, and now, maddened by different emotions, the lust of conquest, the murderous anger over slain companions and, underlying all, the thought of ownership of this fair and warm and safe place of home, were resolute in their attack. They had faith in their leader, Boarface, and expected confidently every moment an onslaught to aid them from above. And so they came up the watery slope, one pressing blood-thirstily behind the other with an earnestness none but men as strong and well equipped and as brave or braver could hope to withstand. The closing struggle was desperate.

Hilltop stood to the front, between two rocks some few yards apart, over which bubbled the shallow creek, and between which was the main upward entrance to the valley. He stood upon a rock almost as flat as i some expert engineer of ages later had plane; its surface and then adjusted it to a level, leaving the shallow waters tumbling all about it. The rock out-jutted somewhat on the slope and there must necessarily be some little climb to face the aged defender. On either side was a stretch of down-running, gradually-sloping waterfall, full of great boulders, embarrassing any straight rush of a group together, but, between and upward, sprang swart men, and facing them on either side of old Hilltop beyond the rocks were the remainder of the mass of cave men upon whom he depended for making good the defense of the whole barrier. Beside him, in the center of the battle, were the two creatures in the world upon whom he could most depend, his stalwart and splendid sons, Strong-Arm and Branch. With them, as gallant if not as strong as his great brother, stood braced the eager Bark. They were ready, these young men, but, as it chanced, there could be, at the beginning of the strong clamber of the foe, only one man to first meet them. All were behind this man at the front, for the flat rock came to something like a point. He stood there, hairy and bare except for the skin about his hips, and with only an ax in his hand, but this did not matter so much as it might have done, for only axes were borne by the up-clambering assailants. The throwing of an ax was a little matter to the sharp-eyed and flexile-muscled cave men. Who could not dodge an ax was better out of the way and out of the world. A meeting such as this impending must be a matter only of close personal encounter and fencing with arm and wooden handle and flint-head of edge and weight.

There was a clash of stone together, and, one after another, strong creatures with cloven skulls toppled backward, to fall into the babbling creek, their blood helping to change its coloring. Leaping from side to side across his rock, along each edge of which the water rushed, old Hilltop met the mass of enemies, while those who passed were brained by his great sons or by those behind. But the forces were unequal and the plane in front was not steep enough nor the water deep enough to prevent something like an organized onslaught. With fearful regularity, uplifted and thrown aside occasionally in defense to avoid a stroke, the ax of Hilltop fell and there was more and more fine fighting and fine dying. On either side were men doing scarcely less stark work. Hilltop's two sons, on either side of him now, as the assailants, crowded by those behind, pressed closer, fully justified their parentage by what they did, and Bark was like a young tiger. But the onslaught was too strong. There were too many against too few. There were loud cries, a sudden impulse and, though axes rose and fell and more men tumbled backward into the water, the rock was swept upon and won and the old man stood alone amid his foes, his sons having been carried backward by the pressure of the mass. There was sullen battling on the upper level, but there was no fray so red as that where Hilltop, old as he was, swung his awful ax among the close crowding throng of enemies about him. Four fell with skulls cleanly split before a giant of the invaders got behind the gray defender of the pass. Then an ax came crashing down and old Hilltop pitched forward, dead before he fell into the cool waters of the pool below.

There was a yell of exultation from the upward-climbing Eastern cave men as they saw the most dangerous of their immediate enemies go down, but, before the echoes had come back, the sound was lost in that which came from the height above them. It was loud and threatening, but not the yell of their own kind.

There had come sweeping down the valley the victors in the fight at the Eastern end. Ab, with the lust of battle fully upon him as he heard the wild shriek of Moonface, who had seen her husband fall, was a creature as hungry for blood as any beast of all the forest, and his followers were scarce less terrible. Swift and dreadful was the encounter which followed, but the issue was not doubtful for a moment. The barrier's living defenders became as wild themselves as were these conquering allies. The fight became a massacre. Flying hopelessly up the valley, the remnant, only some twenty, of the Eastern cave men ran into the vacant big cave for refuge and there, barricaded, could keep their pursuers at bay for the time at least.

There was no immediate attack made upon the remnant of the assailants who had thus sought refuge. They were safely imprisoned, and about the cave's entrance there lay down to eat and rest a body of vengeful men of twice their number. The struggle was over, and won, but there was little happiness in the Fire Valley which had been so well defended.

Moonface, wildly fighting, had seen her husband's death. With the rush of Ab's returning force which changed the tide of battle she had been swept away, shrieking and seeking to force herself toward the rock whereon old Hilltop had so well demeaned himself. Now there emerged from one side a woman who spoke to none but who clambered down the rough waterway and waded into the little pool below the rock and stooped and lifted something from the water. It was the body of the brave old hunter of the hills. With her arms clutched about it the woman began the clamber upward again, shaking her head dumbly, when rude warriors, touched somehow, despite the coarse texture of their being, came wading in to assist her with the ghastly burden. She emerged with it upon the level and laid it gently down upon the grass, but still uttered no word until her children gathered and the weeping Lightfoot came to her and put her arms about her, and then from the uncouth creature's eyes came a flood of tears and a gasp which broke the tension, and the death wail sounded through the valley. The poor, affectionate animal was a little nearer herself again.

There were dead men lying beside the flames at the Eastern end of the valley, and these were brought by the men and tossed carelessly into the pools below where lay so many others of the slain.   There were storm clouds gathering and all the valley people knew what must happen soon. The storm clouds burst; the little creek, transformed suddenly into a torrent by the fall of water from the heights above, swept the dead men away together to the river and so toward the sea.   Of all the invading force there remained alive only the three who had re-leaped the flames and those imprisoned in the cave.

There was council that night between Ab and his friends and, as the easiest way of disposing of the prisoners in the cave, it was proposed to block the entrance and allow the miserable losers in battle to there starve at their leisure. But the thoughtful Old Mok took Ab aside and said:

"Why not let them live and work for us? They will do as you say.   This was the place they wanted.   They can stay and make us stronger."

And Ab saw the reason of all this and the hungry, imprisoned men were given the alternative of death or obedient companionship. They did not hesitate long. The warmth of the valley and its other advantages were what they had come for and they had no narrow views outside the food and fuel question. The valley was good. They accepted Ab's authority and came out and fed and, with their wives and children, who were sent for, became of the valley people.

This place of refuge and home and fortress was acquiring an importance.

CHAPTER XXX.

OUR VERY GREAT GRANDFATHER.

AND the years passed. One still afternoon in autumn a gray, hairy man, a man approaching old age, but without weakness of arm or stiffness of joint, as yet, sat on the height overlooking the village. He looked in tranquil comfort, now down into the little valley, and now across it into the wood beyond, where the sun was approaching the treetops. He had come to the hill with the mere instinct of the old hunter seeking to be completely out of doors, but he had brought work with him and was engaged, when not looking thoughtfully far away, in finishing a huge bow, the spring of which he occasionally tested. Every motion showed the retained possession of tremendous strength as well as the knowledge of its use to most advantage. A very hale old man was Ab, the great hunter and head of the people of the Fire Valley.

A few yards away from Ab, leaning against the trunk of a beech, stood Lightfoot, her quick glance roving from place to place and as keen, seemingly, as ever. These two were still most content when together, and it was well for each that they had in the same degree withstood what the years bring. The woman had, perhaps, changed less than the man. Her hair was still dark and her step had not grown heavy. She had changed in face and expression rather than in form. There had grown in her eyes and about her mouth the indefinable lines and tokens, pathetic and sweet, of care, of sorrow, of suffering and of quiet gladness, in short, of motherhood.

As twilight came on the woods rang with the shouts and laughter of a party of young men who were coming home from some forest trip. Ab, looking down the valley, over the flashing flame, into the forest hills, in whose deep shade lay Little Mok, old Hilltop and Ab's mother, could see the lusty youths in the village, running, leaping, wrestling and throwing spears, axes and stones in competition. A strange oppression came upon him and he thought of Oak lying in the ground alone on the hillside, miles away. Ab felt, even now, the strong, helpful arm of his friend around him, just as it was in the evening journey from

the Feast of the Mammoth homeward, when
he had been rescued from almost certain death
by Oak.   A lump rose in the throat of the
man of many battles and many trials.   He
shook himself, as if to shake off the memory
that plagued him.   Oak came not often to
trouble Ab's peace now, and when he came it
was always at night.   Morning never found
him near the Fire Village.

The young hunters, rioting like the young
men in the valley, were passing now.   Ab
looked upon them thoughtfully.   He felt
dimly a desire to speak to them, to tell them
something about the hurts they might avoid,
and how hard it was to have a great, heavy
load on one's chest at times—all one's life—
but the cave man was, as to the emotions, in-
articulate.   Ab could no more have spoken
his half defined feelings than the tree could
cry out at the blow of the ax.

The woman left the beech tree and approached the man and touched his arm.   His
eyes turned upon her kindly and after she had
seated herself beside him, there was laughing
talk, for Lightfoot was declaring her desperate
condition of hunger and demanding that he
return to the valley with her.   She examined

his bow critically and had an opinion to express, for so fine a shot as she might surely talk a little about so manful a thing as the making of the weapon. And as the sun sank lower and the valley fell into shadow, the two descended together, a pair who, after all, had reason to be glad that they had lived.

And the children these two left were bold and strong and dominant by nature, and maintained the family leadership as the village grew. With later generations came trouble vast and dire to the people of the land, but it was not the part of this proud and seasoned and well-weaponed group to flee like wild beasts when came drifting to the Westward the first feeble vanguard of the Aryan overflow. The vanguard was overthrown; its men made serfs and its women mothers. Other cave men in other regions might escape to the Northward as the wave increased, there to become frost-bitten Lapps or the "Skrallings" of the Norsemen, the Eskimo of to-day, but not so the people of the great Fire Valley or their stern and sturdy vassals for half a hundred miles about. No child's play was it for those of another and still rude civilization to meet them in their fastnesses, and the end of the struggle—for this region at least—was, not a conquest, but a blending, a blending good for each of the two forces.

And as the face of Nature changed with the ages, as the later glacial cold wavered and fluctuated and forced back and forth migrations of man and beast, still the first-formed group retained coherence, retained it beyond great natural cataclysms, retained it to historic ages, to wield long the smoothed stone weapons, and, afterward, the bronze axes, and to diverge in many branches of contentious defenders and invaders, to become Iberian and Gaul and Celt and Saxon, to fight family against family, and to commingle again in these later times.

Upon the beach the other day, watching the waves lap toward her, sat a woman, cultured, very beautiful and wise in woman's way and among the fairest and the best of all earth can produce. There are many such as she. Barely longer ago than the other day, as time is counted, a rugged man, gentle as resolute and noble, became the enshrined hero of a vast republic, when he struck from slave limbs the shackles of four million people. In an insular home across the sea, interested still in the world's affairs, is an old man vigorous in his octogenarianism, a power, though out of power, a figure to be a monument in personal history, a great man. But a few years ago the whole world stood with bowed head while into the soil he loved was lowered the coffin of one who has bound the nations together in sympathy for *Les Miserables* of the earth. In a home on the continent broods watchfully a bald-headed giant in cavalry boots, one who has dictated arbitrarily, as premier, the policy of the empire he has largely made. The woman upon the sands, the great liberator, the man wonderful even in old age, the heart-stirring writer, the man of giant personality physical and mental, have had reason to boast alike a strain of the blood of Ab and Lightfoot. In the veins of each has danced the transmitted product of the identical corpuscles which coursed in the veins of those two who first found a home in the Fire Valley. Strong was primitive man; adroit, patient and faithful was primitive woman; he, the strongest, she, the fairest and cleverest of the time, could protect their offspring, breed and care for great children of similar powers and so insure a lasting race.

Thus has the good blue blood come down. This is not romance, this is not fancy; this is but faithful history.

THE END

www.ingramcontent.com/pod-product-compliance
Lightning Source LLC
Chambersburg PA
CBHW060350260626
47160CB00006B/2263